A Shoul(

A Nov

Published by Michelle Stimpson
http://www.MichelleStimpson.com
Edited by April Barker
Cover art by Kimberly Killion
http://thekilliongroupinc.com

Acknowledgments

I bless God for the gift of writing. It is my honor to give it back to Him.

I'm thankful to all of my readers who have, for almost ten years now, been so gracious to buy and review my books over and over again. We've been through some serious stuff!

Special thanks to my agent, Sara Camilli, for allowing me to pick her brain about the content of this book. Also, thanks to April for a listening ear and for editing. You are such a blessing to my life!

Thanks to my normal, regular, loving husband who went so far as to hand-wash dishes so I could finish writing this book! LOL! Love you, babe!

I'm off to the next book now!

Chapter 1

Dear Me,

Another day, another dollar that seems like only fifty cents. Been working here almost two years, temp-to-perm. Still earning the temp pay, though, because they claim like there's a salary freeze.

This is not the government. Never heard of a salary freeze in the corporate world.

I know I should be glad to have a job in this economy, but these people are working my nerves.

But maybe it's not the people. Maybe it's me. I don't know.

-Chaka

My lunch break was over. *Return to foolishness.* I snapped the rubber band around my journal, then backed my seat away from the table, scraping the 1970s white tile with the legs of a chair that was probably even older. The entire break room probably hadn't been updated since before I was born, if ever. One of these days, someone who'd gotten fired would probably call the city and have the building condemned. Those leaky ceiling tiles coupled with exposed wires could result in at least a week off from work—hopefully not the week of the 15th or the 30th, though. I couldn't afford a delay in payday.

"Hey, Chaka-Chaka." My co-worker, Felecia, pranced in like somebody who'd just gotten a pony for her birthday. I didn't like the way she always said my first name twice, real fast.

But at least she wasn't calling me completely out of my name: Chaka Kahn, Shaka Zulu, Chaka-Rocka. I heard it all growing up.

"Hi, Felecia. How are you?"

"I'm good. How was your weekend?"

"Same as usual," I moaned, joining her at the sink to rinse out my plastic container.

"Oh, what did you pack?" she asked, obviously trying to decipher the remains of my lunch.

Why is she always so nosy? "Lasagna."

"Homemade?"

"Yep." *Some of us can't afford to go out to eat every five minutes.*

"Wow! Do you cook for your family every night?" Felecia asked, drying her dish with a plastic towel and placing it back in the community cabinet.

That's just nasty, sharing dishes with the whole office. Ain't enough Palmolive and hot water in the world to make me use the same plate as fifteen other people. That's why I had to hold my tongue and keep my temper in check because if I went to the penitentiary, I would've starved.

"Do you?" she prodded.

"Do I what?"

"Do you cook every night?"

I must have been so distracted by her repulsive act that I got lost in a trance thinking about all those germs still alive and breathing on the plate. "I cook about four nights a week. My boys are getting to the age where a Happy Meal just makes them mad."

Felecia bent so far over laughing I could see the tracks at the top of her head. "Oh my gosh! You are so funny! You could be like, the cooking comedian."

If she weren't my boss's niece, I would have had to tell her something. But Felecia was the type who'd probably have a meltdown if someone told her to stop with all the cheerfulness.

Life was not that good, in my opinion.

"What's on the Christmas menu?" she interrogated all the more.

I reached past her for a paper towel to finish my cleaning routine. "A ham. Dressing. Greens. The usual."

Felecia crossed her arms and settled her skinny behind against the counter. Another no-no. "Man, Chaka-Chaka. Your life is so awesome. You've got a husband, two beautiful kids. I'll bet they love it when you cook for them. This time of year, I get completely jealous of people like you, with families." The glazed look in her eyes told me she wasn't joking. She sighed and continued the revelry, "Opening Christmas presents together. Singing Christmas carols around the piano."

I held up my right hand. "Okay, you can stop right there. We don't sing. We get up, we have a word of prayer, we open the boxes, the kids add up all the money from their gift cards. My husband and I go back to bed until I get up again around eleven to finish cooking."

A goofy smile spread across her face. "That's beautiful."

"No, it's not. It's just normal. What's up with your family?" *She must have been raised in an orphanage or something.*

"I was raised in a girls' home."

Oh, snap!

"Until my Aunt Julie found me and took me in, when I was thirteen. By then, all I wanted was money for Christmas."

Now, I felt bad for the girl. But I wasn't one to get into people's sob stories. I had enough problems of my own to deal with. "I'm sorry for your difficult childhood. You're right, though. Once kids approach the teen years, they do value the dollar."

I eased my way right out of that one without getting too personal. I walked back to the table, pushed my chair in, and grabbed my purse. "Talk to you later."

"Okay," Felecia chirped.

I stopped off in the restroom to floss my teeth. After finishing that task, I checked myself in the mirror. My hair, which sprouted out all around my face, made for a wavy backdrop to my best features—naturally arched eyebrows, thick lips, and high cheekbones.

Too bad no one could really appreciate the rest of my facial structure underneath the extra padding on my face. I couldn't be sure if it was because of the extra pounds or gravity that my face got rounder and rounder each year.

My sister, Chakira, said if I did these crazy facial exercises she forwarded to me, I could build up the muscles of my face and keep my youthful profile. But those chin-lifts and mouth-clinches hurt! Gave me a headache. I'd have to learn to love my stocky cheeks.

On my way down the main hallway, a twinge of guilt rose inside me. I knew I shouldn't have been so…what's the word for it, distant? Detached? Anti-social? I just couldn't see myself getting all personal with the people on my job because it was simply that—a *job*. We were co-workers, not best friends. The less I fraternized with them, the less drama I could expect. Probably wouldn't earn any brownie points with my boss, but what did it matter? So long as the direct deposit showed up like clockwork, I really didn't care.

From the way Felecia talked, she was probably only two questions away from inviting herself to my house on Christmas Day. *I don't think so.*

I stepped into my office and closed the door behind me. The desk, computer, scanning machine, and visitor's chair were waiting to start another round of appointments with people filing bankruptcy. My job at the law firm was to first verify that they'd brought all of the documents, then scan them into their digital files so the paralegals and attorneys could take it from there.

My one o'clock appointment, a teacher who was married to a doctor, had the nerve to bring in their dog.

"Oh, no. He has to go," I told her the moment she stepped into my world with that fluff ball that was probably already shedding its white hair in my space. About to make me bring in a vacuum.

The client looked at me, bewildered. She huffed twice, then flicked her brown hair behind her shoulders. "No one at the *front* said anything to me."

"Mrs. Kabara, this is a place of business for humans. Animals are not allowed here."

"There's no posted sign anywhere in or around this building," she countered. "Lawyers should know that if you don't want dogs in the building, you have to post a sign."

"Restaurants don't have *no-dog* signs, either, but you wouldn't take him into IHOP, would you?"

She bunched up her bird-lips and squinted her beady eyes at me. "I wouldn't be caught dead eating at IHOP."

"Yap! Yap!" The little monster must have sensed his master getting upset.

And in popped Clarence. God knows I could not stand him. "Is there a problem?" he asked.

Mrs. Kabara answered for the both of us, "This young lady is telling me Juniper has to leave."

"That is correct," I seconded.

Clarence winked at Mrs. Kabara. "Um, Chaka, could I have a word with you in private?" He motioned for me to step outside my office.

I hoisted my purse again on my shoulder as I met him ten feet down the hallway.

Clarence's toupee was tilted ever-so-slightly to the right, giving it the beret effect. "Chaka, this is Mrs. Ka-ba-ra," he enunciated with bugged, blue eyes. "Wife of Dr. Iago Ka-ba-ra."

"I don't care if she's the wife of Dr. Cum-ba-*ya*, she cannot bring a dog into my office. I'll be sneezing all afternoon. Plus, it's unprofessional. This is a place of business." I was doing my best to keep this conversation between only the two of us, but already I could see heads bobbing out of their offices.

"The Kabaras are *very* influential in the community," he shot back.

I understood his position. Money talks, especially to lawyers. "They can't be too influential. They are filing chapter thirteen."

Clarence whispered, "They're far from broke. We're just trying to save what they've earned."

This was code language for trying to dodge paying overdue taxes or a significant amount of child support based on actual income. Deadbeat parents and deadbeat citizens—my least favorite clients. Somehow, they just didn't get that they were supposed to live on less, like the rest of us.

"Look, if you want to take the dog into *your* office and keep it there while I scan her documents, knock yourself out."

He heaved through of his nostrils. "Fine."

I led the way back to my office. Mrs. Kabara was seated in the extra chair with Juniper in her lap.

"Mrs. Kabara, Clarence is willing to watch the dog while you and I continue with our meeting," I politely informed her. In fact, I was quite proud of my especially pleasant demeanor.

She looked straight past me, to Clarence. "I'd like to be seen by someone else, please."

"Yap! Yap!" Juniper backed her up.

"Well," Clarence coughed, "unfortunately…um…Chaka is the only one who can scan for you. Our other assistant, Stacy, is on her lunch break now. They rotate."

"Is Stacy in the building?" Mrs. Kabara pressed.

"She is on. Her. Break," I reiterated. "You're welcome to come back at two o'clock. Perhaps she can see you and Juniper then."

"Who's in charge here?" the client demanded to know.

"Um-uh-that's…let me, um…" Clarence stuttered.

"Attorney Katherine Waymire. 214-555-2287. Her secretary will answer," I gladly informed Mrs. Kabara. I swear, if I were one of those neck-rolling, mouth-smacking sisters, she would have gotten every ounce she deserved. I never could make my neck lean right, though.

"Mrs. Kabara, don't bother Attorney Waymire," Clarence intervened. He held out a hand, helping the client up from the chair. "I'll give Stacy a call on her cell phone and get her back in asap. Follow me."

And with that, Clarence led Mrs. Kabara and that yelping overpriced rug out of my workspace.

I don't have time for this, Lord.

Chapter 2

I should have known. They'd probably been looking for a reason to fire me anyway. In the two years I worked at the law firm, I had never once been employee of the month despite the fact there were no more than fifteen people working there at a time.

What I never understand was why they couldn't have fired me before I went on my lunch break the next day. *Don't have me go to lunch, come back, and then tell me I'm fired. Fire me early, so I can take my time eating my lunch!*

"We'll mail your personal belongings to you," Clarence was all-too-eager to inform.

"Okay."

He slid an envelope across the wood table. "Here's your severance pay."

Knowing Clarence, he probably thought I was supposed to say "thank you."

He stood, so I followed his cue and walked toward the door.

"Chaka," he called out.

I pivoted. Faced him.

"Off the record, I think it's important for you to understand—"

"Don't tell me anything off the record," I spared him. "Goodbye."

Shoot, I was off the clock. I wasn't going to sit there and let him lecture me when I wasn't getting paid to endure it.

On the way to the car, I tried offering myself comforting thoughts. *They can take this stupid job and stick it where the sun don't shine! They never paid me what I was worth, anyway! It's probably the best thing— their loss, not mine!* But the moment I snapped myself into the seatbelt, I let out a frustrating scream.

"URGHHHHH! What now?!"

I reached into my purse and opened the envelope with my extra check. Two weeks' worth of pay. *Was that all I meant to them?* Why would they fire me over a dog? If a rough-looking man had waltzed into the office with a pit bull, there's no way they would have allowed him past the reception area.

But Mrs. Kabara, wife of *Dr.* Kamara who was hiding money overseas, well, she and her loud-mouthed yapping Juniper get special treatment.

People like her, with money and clout, always got special treatment even when they were trying to do the wrong thing. *It's not fair.*

I came home to an empty apartment, which unnerved me somewhat. I couldn't remember the last time I'd been home alone. *Anywhere* alone, for that matter. If I wasn't with the kids and/or Byron, I was at work. If I wasn't at work, I was at Momma's. If not at Momma's, I was at church or maybe the grocery store.

An empty, quiet apartment seemed foreign. I still had five hours before it was time for me to report to my part-time, seasonal employment at Goldberg's Jewelry store. I didn't know what to do with myself without someone yelling "Momma!" or asking, "Chaka, can you…?"

I plopped down on the living room couch of our two-bedroom apartment, taking a long hard look at my surroundings.

From where I was seated, I could see 75% of everything Byron and I had to our name. Family room furniture that didn't match. A 42-inch television screen in an almost-wood entertainment center and a video game system I had never played. Two old-school halogen lamps. The plant the church sent for Daddy's funeral two winters ago. Every time it got close to dying, I pruned it, watered it, and brought it back to life.

A shoelace sprouting from underneath the coffee table caught my attention. I bent over and drug the shoe from its hiding place. Only yesterday, London had been looking for this shoe and I *told* him he'd left it somewhere in the living room.

He had come running back to me in the kitchen. "I can't find it."

"Did you look?"

"Yes, I looked," he insisted.

"Did you look *hard*?"

"Yes," he'd sulked. "I can't find my Superman high-tops anywhere."

"Well, that's too bad. I'm busy cooking. Ask your brother or your Daddy to help you. If you'd put your stuff up where it belongs, you wouldn't have this problem."

London had sat down at the kitchen table and cried for a good ten minutes. His reaction to disappointment was always over-the-top, a symptom of him being mildly autistic.

I took the shoe in hand and walked toward the boys' room. London would be ecstatic when he saw his precious shoe in its place. Too bad I wouldn't be here when the boys got home.

I opened their bedroom door and braced my senses. Now that they boys were ten and twelve, somehow, their living quarters always managed to keep a slightly musty odor. Despite how many times Byron and I taught both London and Corey how to wash properly and use deodorant, their bedroom still had a smell I couldn't quite identify.

"They're just boys," my mother had said. "It comes with the territory."

I could hardly wait for the first little girl to catch Corey's eye. Maybe then, he'd have a motive to become meticulous about his hygiene.

But who was I kidding? Their father wasn't the cleanest chap around, either, according to the things I'd witnessed in the laundry.

After putting a few misplaced clothing items back in order, I breathed the fresh air as I walked the seven steps to my own bedroom. It was hard to believe that, after eleven years of marriage, Byron and me were still using the same bedroom suit my father bought me when I turned sixteen years old. The white composite-wood with gold trim princess headboard had been my wish for almost two years before Daddy made it come true.

A part of me wanted to keep it forever. I'd often dreamt about giving it to a daughter, the one I never had. But now—at age thirty-two—I was fairly sure I had no business romping around with my husband in a present I'd received half my life ago.

I wished we could afford better. Not just for us, but for the boys, too. Corey's feet were hanging off the end of his twin bed every night.

I kicked off my heels and set them side-by-side in front of the dresser so they'd be ready to roll when it was time to head to Goldberg's.

The mirror across from me told no lies. I was gaining weight again. Not enough to bust out of my size 14's, but enough to make me pass on the desserts for the rest of the week.

Why couldn't I be one of those people with super-fast metabolisms? My college roommate, Nancy McGregor, ate like a pig and never gained an ounce. She said it was in her genes. Her mom and her aunts shared this same glorious chromosome.

Some people have it so easy.

My cell phone rang. I grabbed it from my cardigan pocket. *Byron.* "Hello?"

"Hey. Did you pay the insurance yet?"

"No," I said.

"Okay. Don't pay it until I get my check Friday."

"There *should* be enough in the bank for me to pay it today," I tested him.

"Should be, but there's not. So don't pay it. We can't afford any overdraft fees."

Now he wants to avoid overdraft fees. He's the overdraft king! "What happened to the money, Byron?"

"Wait—wait. Hold on. Let me call you right back." He ended the call abruptly.

I didn't waste any time opening the bank app on my phone and logging in to view the latest activity in our account. "Four hundred and thirty-seven dollars at Kindall's Wholesale!" I shouted to no one in particular. "Mmm mmm. No he did not."

I called him back. Got voice mail. "Byron, call me back. Now!"

My heart beat double-time as I stared at my own blank expression in the mirror. "Really?"

It's a good thing he called right away because my next step would have been to go to his job. "What is this four hundred dollar purchase at Kindall's?"

"Baby," he started, which I already recognized as foolishness, "you know I've been having my eye on a set of rims—"

"Rims as in *car* rims?!"

"Yeah. For the Mustang. They had 'em on sale. Discontinued, almost next to nothing—"

"Take the rims back! No, I'll take them back for you! Where are they?" I got up and searched his side of the closet.

"They're custom, being sent to me,"

"Even better. You can stop the order," I informed him.

"No, I couldn't if I wanted to—which I don't. They're already on their way. Should be here in a couple of weeks."

"And the minute they get here, we're sending them right back," I said.

"Chaka, by that time, we'll both have gotten a few more checks. It'll be okay."

"No, it's not okay! I'm working two jobs—two jobs— to get us through the holiday season. And here you are buying rims for an old, beat-up Mustang that's sitting in our second parking spot covered with a tarp!"

He shouldn't have gotten me started on that car.

"Calm down. Look, I'm not taking the rims back. And nobody told you to get another job. You're the one always trying to keep up with the Joneses," he took a jab.

"Well, my maiden name is Jones, remember?" I reminded him.

"Anyway, I need you to stop worrying. Everything will be fine. It always is," he tried to calm me.

"It's not fine, Byron! Nothing is fine! We're always broke! Every time I look around, we've got a late fee for this, a disconnect notice for that! We're too *old* to still be living paycheck to paycheck! I'm tired of it!" Emotion squeaked through my voice.

"Baby, calm down," he whispered. "What's wrong?"

I sniffed, wiping my eyes. "I got fired today."

He whistled sharply. "Man. Babe. That's crazy."

"I know, right?"

He asked, "What happened?"

"Politics. They wanted me to allow a woman with her dog into my office and I wouldn't. Ridiculous."

"You like dogs, though?" he ventured.

"You know I don't believe dogs belong indoors," I reminded him.

"Mmm."

"It wasn't just about the dog, though," I thought out loud. "Since the economy is picking back up, we haven't had as many people filing bankruptcy. It was only a matter of time before they had to let someone go, probably."

"One man's dream is another man's nightmare," Byron sighed. "Maybe you could try to go full-time at Goldberg's. You said, yourself, that you could make pretty good money if you were there forty hours a week. Unlimited earning potential."

He had a point. He didn't have much money or any sense of priority, but he did have this optimistic attitude thing going for him.

"Those rims are still going back."

"If we have to, yeah, but I don't think we'll have to," he kept hope alive.

"We'll see. I'll talk to you later."

"Babe," he reached out to me again, "don't worry. It'll all work out. Isn't that what Pastor Dale preached about the other Sunday? All things work together for our good?"

My husband had a knack for getting real religious when the going got tough. "For the good of them who love the Lord and are called according to His purpose. Still doesn't change the fact that when those rims were calling you, you shouldn't have answered the phone!"

"Yeah. All that," Byron agreed blindly. "I gotta go."

"Bye."

Still couldn't believe I'd been fired. Or that my husband had spent four hundred dollars on rims. No, I take that back. The rims I could believe. For some reason, Byron was dead-set on reviving that 1998 convertible Mustang from the outside in. "When we get some extra money, I'm gonna fix it up. You'll see."

He'd said that three years ago when an elderly woman totaled my parked car and we got a check for $4500 from her insurance company. We'd used half to buy the Mustang, the other half to put down on my car. It was our first and only windfall and once I learned that the lady hadn't suffered injuries, I was grateful. That was the most money I'd ever seen on a check made out to me.

I took a picture of it on my phone, thinking I'd never see such a sight again. So far, I had been right.

I lay back on the bed and stared up at the frosted light cover. Cheap. Everything in this room (except what my father bought) was cheap. Our clothes, our shoes, the curtains, the paintings tacked to the walls.

My husband was cheap. Even though four hundred dollars was a lot of money to me for rims, he'd said they were dirt cheap on clearance.

Maybe the only things I could call mine that hadn't come cheap was London. Corey, our oldest, had been "free" because, as an unmarried college student, I was (to the government) another single mom with no income. Medicaid had covered my doctor bills, the hospital bills and his medical needs for a year afterward. I think I might have paid $150 to the anesthesiologist who had administered the epidural, and Lord knows he was worth every penny.

While Corey was still in diapers, I made the decision to go to a rinky-dink for-profit school and earn a certificate as an administrative assistant. Little did I know, for as much as I borrowed to "start a career in nine months!" I could have darn near finished my college degree. *Why do they even allow such highway robbery?*

By the time we had London, we were married. I had dropped out of college and joined Byron in the workforce. We had each other's income and a little bit of insurance, which meant we had to pay a lot out of pocket. Took us almost six years to pay off all those bills, then we got another round when London was diagnosed with autism. If it hadn't been for the Autism Speaks organization, we wouldn't have been able to get him any help.

He was better now. Much better. Maybe, one day, he'd even be able to move out of the apartment and live his own life.

What about me? Will I ever leave this apartment? Move into a house? Have a real life? Not if it depended on my income as an administrative assistant and Byron's wages as a dockworker at Jefferson-Giles Transportation. Both of us worked full-time. Never could get ahead of the game, though. *If only I had finished my English degree.*

I rested my eyes for a second, like my Daddy used to do when the assistant pastor preached at church. I would poke Daddy in the side and ask, "Are you sleeping in church?"

And he would say, "No, Chaka. I'm just restin' my eyes."

Laughter rippled through me. Daddy knew good and well he was falling asleep on the sermon.

Those were good times.

I knew I couldn't change the past, but it certainly was nice to remember how things were when I didn't have a care in the world. No impulsive husband, no needy kids, no disappointment, no taking one step forward and two steps back. No getting fired.

I felt a tear trickle from the corner of my eyes back into my hairline.

If I could do it all over again.

Chapter 3

I used the rest of my free time constructively by catching up on recorded episodes of the Real Housewives from three different cities. They had drama and issues, of course, but still…they were rich. They were used to being home alone, like I was that afternoon. They had plenty of free time to work out, shop, and have lunch with friends in the middle of the workday.

Beyond the glamour, they had *lives*. Business ventures, product lines, non-profit organizations. The really cool part was that most of them came from modest backgrounds. They weren't any smarter than me, but somehow they had made different choices and they were on top. On television, on magazine covers. Their families were proud of them—who wouldn't be? They'd made it. *Why couldn't I have been a Real Housewife of Somewhere?*

After spending three and a half hours watching their exciting lives unfold, I tore myself away from the television and sank back down to my reality. It was time to go to work and try to sell diamonds I could never afford.

For the second time that day, I felt like crying. *My life is nothing but an extended workday.* Between my husband, the boys, and busting my buns at jobs, what else did I have? *Why isn't my life exciting and fulfilling?*

Movement outside the window caught my eye. The woman upstairs was descending with another lady. Both were dressed stylishly, with bouncing, flowing hair to compliment. It was four-thirty in the afternoon and they were heading off to do something fun, presumably. Must have taken them an hour or so to get ready.

How do they get to do leisurely things all day?

Either I was in the wrong profession or the wrong life altogether.

My shoes were waiting for me at the dresser, but before I put them on, I made a pit stop in my closet. I tiptoed and managed to scoot a cardboard box to the edge just above my head. One hop up and I was able to pull it down.

This box, this treasure, was my time capsule. My joy. I didn't open it often, but when I did, a flood of memories overtook me and reminded me of what it was like to live with hope and expectation. Back when teachers and parents would say, "You can be anything you want to be when you grow up." Back when anything was possible.

The old filing box contained six journals dating back to my freshman year of high school. As was my custom when I visited the old diaries, I searched for the entry closest to the exact date ten and fifteen years ago and relived wherever I was back then.

Only ten years earlier, I had written:

There's something going on with the baby, but everybody keeps telling me not to compare London to Corey. No two children are the same. I get that. But there's something else. When I tried to explain it to the doctor, he kept saying not to worry. Am I paranoid? Am I crazy? Am I sleep-deprived? Maybe all three. I don't know.

A tear fell from my cheek onto the paper. I knew London was different, but no one would listen. I could have kicked myself for not listening to my instincts. If we had intervened sooner, things might be different.

I could drive myself crazy reading the problems I wrote about when the boys were little. Good thing I didn't have much time to write during those years. I closed that journal, opting for happier memories.

Fifteen years before, I was seventeen.

THIS IS THE BEST DAY OF MY LIFE!!! Me and Myeisha are going to the Brandy concert with Calvin and L.A.! We are going to meet them up there since my mom won't let us ride in the car with them. Why does she have to be so strict????? Anyway, it doesn't matter. I always get my way. Why? Because I'm tha bomb!

Myeisha dyed her hair and her mom almost wasn't going to let her go to the concert because she didn't ask her mom. But then Myeisha asked her mom how could she get in trouble for something her mom never told her she couldn't do. Her mom let her off punishment!!!

That wouldn't have happened with my mom. She is so unreasonable.

I think I'm going to wear my blue jean jumper with a pink sweatshirt and my Timberland boots.

I am so excited. Calvin finally broke up with Alexis for good this time. Her hair is so fried. I don't know why he likes her anyway. I did my best to impress him, and it finally paid off. Don't know what it is, but when I am around him, I feel like I could float to the sky! This is true love.

But, if I see somebody who looks better at the concert, I don't know what I will do. Ha! Ha! Ha! My life is so unpredictable and fun!

Those were the good old days.

At my evening gig, the other sales associates and I almost fought over who would get to assist bachelors looking for wedding rings. Those particular men came in with a certain budget in mind, but could easily be convinced that their bride-to-be would appreciate something in a slightly higher range. "This ring is forever," was my favorite line, worth at least another ten dollars in commission.

That night, I spotted him the moment he walked into the store. Tall, dark, and handsome. Clean-shaven, yet he sported a dab of street swag on him. Probably had a tattoo somewhere under that designer suit. I made a beeline and introduced myself to him, "Hello, I'm Chaka."

"Jeffrey."

"Jeffrey, it's nice to meet you."

We shook hands. I led him toward the showcases. "What brings you in tonight?"

"Looking for an engagement ring."

I leaned back, exaggerating my astonishment. "Congratulations! What's the lucky woman's name?" And I meant every word, staring into his dark brown eyes, strong chin.

"Her name is Lauren."

"Well, let's get Lauren a ring." Enough of the theatrics. "Do you have any ideas about cut, karats, metal, setting? Price range?"

He shrugged. "I'm going to have to defer to your expertise, Chaka. The sky's the limit. Nothing's too good for her."

Hey now! That's what I like to hear! However, I'd been working at Goldberg's long enough to know that some people had no idea how high the sky reached at our store.

So, we started in the upper-mid range, looking at a white gold bridal set. One and a quarter karat set with four princess cut diamonds in the center and 110 round brilliant cut diamonds surrounding the center as well as embedded along the shaft. Priced at $3,299.

Jeffrey twirled the ring around between his perfectly manicured index and thumb. "It's pretty. But Lauren…she means the world to me. We've been through so much together."

"Awww. That's so sweet," I cooed.

"You got anything closer to two karats?"

I gulped. "We certainly do." I nearly snatched the cheap-o ring from him, set it back in its place and locked the cabinet with the keys on my spiral wrist-keychain.

He shook his arm a few times, and I watched his diamond-crusted watch come sliding down as he checked the hour. "That's a lovely timepiece."

"It's a Rolex," he said. "My dad got it for me when I finished med school."

"So it's *Doctor* Jeffrey, then?"

"Yeah, but, you know," he tried to blush, "I don't usually say that when I first meet people."

"You certainly have much to be proud of," I complimented him, fighting hard to keep the dollar signs from flashing through my eyes.

"I owe so much of it to Lauren. She's been by me all these years, you know? Raising our daughter while I've been basically married to school."

The twinkle of love for her was so obvious. *Must be nice.*

"I can see why you want the best for her," I sing-songed.

What if I had stayed in college and let Byron raise Corey? I could have matriculated while he parented. We could have made it, like Jeffrey and Lauren.

We strode on to the inner sanctum of the store, the place where few buyers or salespeople enter because, quite frankly, not everyone is in the market for a $7,000-$10,000 ring. I could feel my fellow associates' stares boring into my body as I led Jeffrey toward the top-dollar case. Selling one of these pieces might mean a whole week's worth of commission for us part-timers, or so I'd heard. I had no first-hand knowledge because this was my first time snagging a big spender.

Jeffrey was a few steps ahead of me when the sparkle of a classic marquis diamond with a cluster of round, shiny friends caught his eye. Two karat. Priced at $8500. "That's the one," he said without wavering.

I wasn't the best at math, but that bad boy was about to knock off my pre-paid cell phone bill for the month or even more, if he bought the lifetime care plan. "Wow! You've already decided?"

"I know what I want when I see it. That's it," he pointed at the ring.

"Perfect." I entered the code on the secure half-door (which made no sense) and then approached the backside of the counter to insert my key while Jeffrey extracted a credit card from his wallet.

I jammed the key into the slot, but it wouldn't turn. *Must be the wrong key.* I tried the next one. The third key wouldn't fit, either. "Um…just a moment," I said to Jeffrey. My heart's pace quickened. I had a humongous one on the line and I needed to reel him in quickly, before he looked at the other, cheaper pieces.

Without even thinking about it, I flagged down the nearest sales associate, Paul. He was a retired school principal who had, reportedly, been working at the store for almost three years. If anyone knew how to open this revered jewelry box, Paul would. He cool-cat-daddy-limped on over to us. "Yes?"

"Hi, Paul, I'm trying to show one of the rings in this cabinet, but my key won't work.

"Wonderful." He turned to my customer. "Hi, I'm Paul. Which ring do you have in mind?"

Jeffrey indicated his choice.

Paul's face lit up. "A man with exquisite taste!" He looked at me. "Let me just come around and help you with this, Chaka."

Already, I knew Paul was trying to work his way in on my deal, so I did a James Brown slide away from Jeffrey and met Paul as soon as he entered the secured area. "All I need you to do is unlock the case, my brother."

He breezed past me, toward Jeffrey and the rings. "Be glad to help."

Paul unlocked the sliding door with ease. He reached in and pulled out the ring.

I grabbed it from him mid-air. "Thank you, Paul. You've been most helpful." I gave him a fake smile and a slight jerk of the head.

Paul completely ignored my cues for him to leave. Instead, he stood there as I oooh-ed and aaah-ed the ring with Jeffrey and expounded on the various features of the ring.

"It's amazing," Jeffrey agreed. The platinum credit card still resting in his palm.

"She'll love it. Let me just grab a customization form so that we can get it sized." I stepped away for just a second to get the paperwork. That was all the space Paul needed.

"Now, did Chaka tell you about our lifetime care plan?" He leaned an elbow onto the case.

I hurried back. "I was just about to, thank you."

Paul lingered. "Well, it's a great ring, and you need a way to protect it. The lifetime care plan will—"

"I've got this, Paul. Thank you."

Jeffrey handed me the ring. I wrote my associate ID number at the top of the page, big and bold and circled it so that Paul could see he would have nothing to do with this here sale. Still, Paul didn't budge.

"Okay, Jeffrey, go ahead and fill out the top portion of the form with your name and address. How soon do you need the ring sized and ready to go?"

"Within the next few weeks." Jeffrey smiled. "I want to propose in the company of our family and friends on Christmas Day."

Again, my heart warmed for Lauren. Christmas proposals are so romantic, so unlike the one I got standing next to Byron in the restroom, holding a positive pregnancy test. "Two lines. I'm pregnant," I had said.

"Then let's get married," followed immediately. No ring, no fanfare. Nothing more than a response to a crisis.

Paul's next words threw all thoughts of romanticism aside. "Have you found *your* ring yet, Jeffrey?"

Jeffrey chuckled. "You know, I haven't even *thought* about my ring."

I jumped in, "You'll definitely want something that complements hers. I've got several I can show you."

Paul chided, "But he needs a *man's* perspective for this one."

"As you can see, Jeffrey already has good taste. I can help him with his band as well when the time comes," I stated. Paul was pushing the limits of my professionalism.

Jeffrey's brows pinched together. "When is the right time for the groom to pick a ring?"

"*After* she says yes," I laughed.

Jeffrey nodded. "Duh! Makes perfect sense."

Paul raised up off the counter and shot me a look that could have stopped a train.

Finally, Jeffrey and I were alone. He completed the documentation, signed up for the lifetime care plan, and even gave me a few referrals. We finished the transaction, he signed, sealing the deal. Just like that, I had earned more in one hour at Goldberg's that I could have earned in a whole day at the law firm.

Thank You, Jesus! Maybe Byron was right. Maybe I needed to focus more on the things Pastor Dale said because getting my biggest sale on one of my worst days had to be some kind of sign from heaven, I guessed.

But the minute Jeffrey walked out of the store, the night manager, Lacy—who was every bit of eighteen years old—called me into her office along with Paul.

As we sat, I noticed she was red with anger. Paul set in the chair next to me. I could have sworn steam was coming from his ears.

"Chaka, we have a problem," Lacy sizzled.

I stared at her without responding.

"Paul says he was trying to make another sale with a customer who just spent almost ten thousand dollars in the store. And you suggested that the customer wait until later to make a second purchase.

"Do you not understand how the retail business works?"

All the adrenaline pumping through me from Jeffrey's sale was still fresh in my veins. You couldn't tell me I wasn't a rock star at that moment. "Of *course* I understand how business works. What I don't understand is why Paul, here, tried to *insert himself* into my sale."

Lacy sat back, apparently in shock. "Your word choice is completely inappropriate."

It took me a moment to gather that she had assigned sexual meaning to my words. "I didn't mean it like *that*."

"Sounds like you did," Paul jumped on the bandwagon. "I will not be subject to sexual harassment on my job."

"Sexual harassment?" I shrieked. "Are we still talking about a ring?"

"I hope so. And I hope you'll get with the program, Chaka," Lacy reprimanded. "We're a *team* here at Goldberg's." She took a deep breath as her normal peachy color returned. "Now, since you've basically—what do you call it—player hated on Paul, I think it's only fair that if the customer returns to buy another ring, you two should try to probably split that commission."

Groom's rings weren't nearly as expensive as the brides'. "Whatever. Fine with me."

"I want half of her commission *tonight*," Paul demanded. "I was the first to tell him about the lifetime care plan."

My mouth dropped open.

Lacy asked, "Is this true?"

"I hadn't reached that point in the sales pitch—"

"But the fact remains. I *did* sell him on it."

"You weren't supposed to do *anything* except open the case for me!" I reminded him.

"Why don't you have a key?" from Lacy.

"That's a good question," I co-signed. I only have these three keys, which Paul, here, gave me when I first started working.

"No. I gave you *four* keys."

I gave two big blinks. "I beg to differ. These are the same keys I've had on this same bracelet for the past two weeks."

He shook his head a little too quickly. Now I understood his game. He had purposely kept the key to the most expensive jewelry so that when I needed it, I'd have to ask for help from someone else—namely him. No wonder he'd been conveniently standing by while I was trying desperately to unlock the case!

I crossed my arms. Settled back in my chair and said to Paul, "I'm onto you."

He sat up straight and pointed at me. He yelled to Lacy, "Sexual harassment!"

"Why would I want *your* old behind?" Blame it on the adrenaline.

Lacy's face reddened. "Chaka, I-I…have to suspend you. Indefinitely."

"Are you kidding me? He's lying! He's the one who—"

She cut me off by standing. "I'll take your keys." Lacy held out her hand.

"Why?" I fumed.

"You're still within your first ninety days of voluntary employment. In Texas, we don't have to specify a reason for releasing you," she quoted some handbook for new managers.

And just like that, I'd managed to get myself fired *twice* in the same day.

"Who does this?!" I yelled at myself on the way home from Goldberg's. "Why is my life so stupid and boring and pointless?"

With tears blurring my eyes, I wished with everything in me that I could erase the past thirteen years. Go back to my high school graduation or my last semester in college, before I ever met Byron. Before I ever got pregnant. Before I had two sons whom I adored but, honestly, wasn't ready to bring into this word. They deserved better.

I cried out to God—if He was listening—telling Him that if I could go back in time, everything would be different. Better. I could have been *somebody*.

Most of all, I wouldn't have been sitting up there crying over losing two jobs that didn't amount to diddly-squat anyway after Uncle Sam took his portion.

I couldn't swipe the tears fast enough. Kleenex was in order.

I reached over to the passenger's side and fished through my purse for a tissue. Inadvertently, the hand on the wheel slid to the right with my body.

I tried to correct. Too much.

Skidding. Sliding. Spinning.

That's all I remember.

Chapter 4

The first thing I noticed was the smell of fresh flowers. Roses. My favorite. Byron must have done something stupid, otherwise why would he be trying to get back in my good graces with enough bouquets to collectively perfume an entire room?

Next, with my eyes still closed, I felt the soft padding beneath my shoulder blades. My hips. My whole body seemed to have sunken into this mattress.

Finally, my vision met with utter confusion. A white duvet comforter. Silver posts on the four corners of the bed. Startled, I sat straight up in this luxurious bed. *Where am I?*

As the room came into focus, its beauty overwhelmed me. Sunlight streamed through the elegant, ivory drapes flowing ten feet from the top of the window to the marble tiled floor. To my left, a Victorian-style sofa and love seat with a table set for tea. To my right, a humongous, stone fireplace, which gave me a peek at the bathroom.

"Good morning, Mrs. Lewis," a woman's voice called from the other side of the fireplace. "I'm sorry. I tried not to disturb you, but I have to get the cleaning done before the children come home. You know how they are," she caroled.

I pulled the bedding closer to my chest. "Who are you?"

The woman, old enough to be my mother, emerged from the bathroom and put a hand on her plump hip. She had kind gray eyes, which eased my fears somewhat. She tisked. "You must have taken one too many of those sleeping pills again. I'll have Ida make you coffee. Black."

"I don't like coffee." This was no secret to anyone who knew me.

She squinted. Tilted her head to the side as though I might not know what I was talking about. "You certainly drank three cups yesterday. Why don't you get dressed and come on down for breakfast." She left the room.

What in the world? Where's Byron?

I felt around the empty side of the bed. My left hand brushed against something hard. Seconds later, I discovered a hot pink journal almost identical to the one I'd written in only the day before—the day I got fired twice.

The first page of the diary read: This diary belongs to Chaka Lewis. If found, please return to Ida Vidalgo. *Ida. She's the one who makes coffee.* Why would anyone give my personal belongings to Ida? And how in the world had someone managed to forge my handwriting perfectly? I mean, they had it down to the i's and t's!

Confused to the core, I opened to the first entry, dated October 7 of that same year.

Dear Me,

I hate football season. No sex. It brings out the worst in Dante, especially this year. They're 1-3 right now. Unless something drastic happens, it's going to be a long, losing season. Dante looks good on the field, but there's only so much he can do when he's surrounded by a bunch of losers.

Kids at the academy tease Michaela and DJ about the fumbles and missed passes. I hate what it does to our family.

-Chaka

October 13

Dear Me,

The team is 2-5. Might as well be walking on eggshells around here. Dante has hurt his shoulder, but he's not saying anything because he wants to play.

-Chaka

November 21

Dante did it again. Worse this time.

The only good news: Jabari put me on a high-protein diet. I've lost six pounds. Woo hoo! Back to normal.

-Chaka

In a flash, I drew the covers back and placed my legs on the floor. *Wait-are those my legs?* They were long. Lean. Sexy. I pointed my toe and watched the muscles pop. Obviously, I had been working out. But when? And what *else* wasn't me?

I ran to the bathroom to examine my reflection. Once my feet crossed the threshold, I could feel the warmth. Heated tiles.

The woman staring back at me was definitely me…only better. My skin was as smooth as a baby's bottom, obviously the result of expensive facials. Features precisely defined. Teeth white as a movie star's. I untied the scarf around my head and a mound of top-quality Brazilian hair came cascading down my back.

I flattened my silk nightgown against my stomach. Smooth, as in no lumps. Touched my breasts. Firm, and at least a cup size larger. I took a peek down my collar and realized they were fake.

I gathered my gown in my fist and turned to the side to examine my profile. I couldn't have weighed more than a hundred and twenty pounds. At my height, that put me at a size a size eight.

I am buff! Jabari has whipped me into shape!

And the wedding ring on my finger—shazaam! Made Lauren's look like it came from the Cracker Jack box.

Still, this was crazy. This bathroom, almost bigger than my apartment. The bedroom. Some woman cleaning up for me. *Why am I worried about someone named Dante?*

Glancing back at my bed, I saw a cell phone plugged into the wall. I figured it must be mine, so I yanked it from the charger, hoping this would give me a clue and connect me back to Byron, London, and Corey.

The device was an iPhone. One of those I'd seen on a recent commercial. I tapped the screen and it came alive. *What's my password?*

I entered my old passwords, but none of them worked. Because I messed up so many times, I had to wait three minutes to try again. On the second go round, somehow I ended up pressing my thumb on the main button for a few seconds and—who could have known?—the thing opened up for me. Of course, this freaked me about because now I knew that my fingerprints were still the same. I was still *me*, just different.

I called Byron's cell phone and thanked God when he answered. "Hello?"

His familiar voice sent another wave of gratefulness through me. Finally, I could make sense of the situation. "Oh my gosh, you have no idea how glad I am to hear your voice," I gushed.

"Who is this?"

"It's me. Chaka."

"Chaka who?"

"*Cha*-ka!"

He laughed. "Chaka-Chaka-Chaka Khan? Chaka-Khan, Chaka-Khan, let me rock you Chaka-Khan!"

Byron *knew* I hated when people made fun of my name. "Why would you sing that song at a time like this?"

"Look, I don't know you, okay? The only Chaka I know is Chaka Khan, and she has no reason to call me."

"But Byron, it's *me*! Your wife!"

"Uuuuuh, lady, you got the wrong Byron. My wife's name is Tya."

"Tya? Tya *Longfield*, from Greater New Hope?"

"Yeah. You know my wife? Is this a joke she's put you up to?" he snickered.

Indignant, I reminded him, "I didn't even know you *liked* Tya. In fact, you said she had a sunk-in forehead and her teeth were too big."

He hesitated. "I'm not sure know what kind of—"

"You sayin' your wife don't have big rabbit teeth?" I cornered him, all grammar aside.

"Lady, I'm hanging up now. Bye."

She does *have big, rabbit teeth!*

I tried calling him back, but he wouldn't answer.

Byron doesn't know me.

Oh my gosh—what about our kids?

The phone allowed me access to London and Corey's school's website. I selected the "Parent Access" icon from the main page, then entered my username, which was our last name with four numbers, and password, to which the system replied, "Incorrect username or password. Try again."

I entered my information again, this time more slowly, but still got the same response. The school's main page gave a contact number, so I called the school and asked to speak to London's teacher, Mrs. Handley.

"I'll transfer you," the operator said.

Thank God!

"This is Mrs. Handley. How can I help you?"

"Mrs. Handley, this is Chaka Stringer, London's mom. I was wondering if—"

"I'm sorry, you must be mistaken. I don't have a *London* in my class."

My heart sank. "You teach fourth grade, right?"

"Yes."

"He's...special-ed. Autistic. Did they move him from your class?" There would be H-E-double-hockey-sticks to pay if they moved my baby without consulting me.

"No. I'm the fourth grade lead teacher and I can tell you right off the bat, we don't have anyone named London in the entire fourth grade. Are you sure you've called the right school?"

I could barely breath. "Yes. Well, no. Thank you."

"Good-bye."

My God. If Byron didn't know me, then Corey and London didn't exist. Were they figments of my imagination? Did anyone know me?

Sadness engulfed me as I reached out for one more lifeline. *214-555-3321.* "Hello?" My mother answered.

I was afraid to speak. "Momma?"

"Hello, Chaka."

I sighed and cried. "Momma! You remember me?"

"What kind of silly question is that to ask your own mother," she fussed. "I should be the one asking you the question, seeing as you never hardly even call me."

"I'm sorry. I've just been—" *Been what? In another life?*

"I know how it is," she made excuses for me. "Every football season, you and the kids have a tough go with Dante. Y'all ought to be used to it by now, though. Cowboys ain't had a good season since Troy Aikman. Need to get rid of Jerry Jones, but let me hush my mouth since Mr. Jones is the one signing your husband's paycheck." She laughed at her own observation.

Unsure of how to respond, I echoed her sentiment. "You're right, Momma."

Nothing was what it used to be. Everything was different. People who were supposed to be alive were nonexistent, which made me wonder: Are people who are supposed to be dead still living?

"Momma, how are things around the house?"

"Oh, same as usual," she sang.

How could I ask my mother if my father was alive without upsetting her no matter what the answer? "Do you…talk to people?"

"Oh, yeah. I have friends. You know, Miss Gracie from next door keep tryin' to come over here and get me to start a garden. I told her I ain't the one for bookin' down on the ground on my hands and knees, getting my nails dirty."

My mother's stay-indoors personality was certainly a welcomed memory, as well as Miss Gracie. "What about…things going on *in* the house?"

"Ain't nothin' going on in the house. Ain't nobody in the house but me."

I slapped my palm against my forehead. Daddy was still gone.

Someone rapped on the door. "Mrs. Lewis?"

"Hold on Momma," I said.

The cleaning lady whispered, "The children are home. Would you like to see them now or should I have them wait until later?"

I snarled my nose. "Of course, I'll see them now."

She nodded.

"Momma, I have to go. The kids are here."

"Wonderful! Let me talk to my grandbabies!"

I heard them walking on the hardwood floors before I saw them. And then, they were standing at my doorway— two of the cutest little kids I'd ever laid eyes on. They both had my nose, my lips. I guessed the girl was four, the boy about seven. They were dressed in their little private school uniforms. Blue sweater with slacks for him. A plaid skirt with, blue cardigan, and white blouse for her.

"Are you feeling okay, Mommy?" the girl, whom I assumed was Michaela asked. She and her brother clung to the housekeeper's side as they waited for an answer.

"Yes, I'm okay. Come on in," I invited them in.

They looked up at the housekeeper, as to ask if it was really safe for them to enter.

"Your mother is fine. It's okay," she assured them.

Cautiously, they stepped toward me, almost in unison. "Hello Mommy," my son said.

With the phone still to my left ear, I reached toward him with my right arm. He flinched. Obviously, he thought I was preparing to strike him.

What kind of mother does he think I am? "Honey, I just want to give you two a hug."

They gave me stiff hugs, their bodies trembling in my embrace.

"Your grandmother is on the phone," I told them. "She'd like to speak to both of you."

Michaela grabbed the line. "Hi, Granny! When can we come to your house again?"

"We miss you!" the boy screamed past Michaela's shoulder. "And tell Aunt Chakira we said hi!"

"Be quiet, DJ. I can't hear what she's saying."

A bossy little thing! She made me smile.

"Uh huh. Uh huh," she said. "Okay. We'll wait for Christmas. We have a present for you. And it's big," Michaela hinted.

"Yes, Granny. It's big. And it is…um...gonna help you with stuff."

I could tell where this conversation was going. If I didn't stop these two, my mother wouldn't have much guessing to do on Christmas morning. I took the phone from Michaela. "Momma, I'll talk to you later."

Now that I had the children's undivided attention, I was hoping to pry a bit into our lives.

"So, DJ, how was school today?"

He clasped his hands behind his back. "Fine."

"And yours, Michaela?"

"Fine."

"Well…what do you guys want to do today?"

They looked at each other, puzzled.

"What do you mean?" Michaela asked.

"I mean, do you want to get some ice cream? Go to a museum? Or just sit here and read a book together?" These were the kinds of activities I imagined stay-at-home moms got to do with their kids. And since I was, apparently, one to sleep until three in the afternoon, I figured I must fall into that category.

"I have gymnastics tonight," Michaela.

"Cool! I can't wait to see you out there tumbling." I rolled my fists in a circular motion.

"But Miss Ida takes me to gymnastics," she informed me. The girl's cheeks were so chubby I could just kiss them!

"I'd love to tag along and watch. I'm so proud of you."

Her eyes twinkled. "Okay, Mommy. You can come. If Miss Ida says it's okay."

Miss Ida ain't the boss of me. "Thank you."

The woman I presumed was Ida waltzed into the room without any ado. "Here you are, Mrs. Lewis. Freshly brewed black coffee. I hear you're having a tough time this afternoon with the medication. Kept you in bed all day."

Ida didn't match my picture of a maid, nor did she look like the personal assistant of a football player's wife. She was probably in her late 40's. Tall with a frame so thin I could see the balls of her shoulders through her knit sweater.

"Children, go to your rooms now," she instructed them. "Your Mommy needs rest."

They scrambled out of the room.

"But I just woke up," I said.

Ida tightened the corners of her mouth. "True, but you know how you are."

No, I don't.

"Have some coffee. Did you take your medicine already?"

"I took too much last night," I said.

"It's a brand new day."

When he opened the top drawer on my nightstand. I could hardly believe my eyes. There had to be at least six or seven prescription bottles in there! "My word! How many pills am I on? What's wrong with me?" I shrieked.

Though Ida tried to shove the drawer closed, I counteracted her puny efforts and snatched the containers from the drawer. One was a sleeping pill. Take one nightly. Another for anxiety, to be taken as needed. Another to be taken for stomach cramps. The rest I'd have to look up online. "Am I dying?" *Not that it matters, since this isn't real.*

Ida laughed, holding the drawer open for me. "No. You're under a lot of stress right now."

I held up one of the unpronounceable medications. "What's this one for?"

She took it from and rolled the bottle from left to right as she read the drug's name out loud. "I believe this one is to counteract the effects of the sleeping pill."

"Let me get this straight. I take a pill at night to help me go to sleep. And then I take another one when I wake up?"

"Pretty much."

I gave her another vial. "And this one?"

She examined it. "This is your appetite suppressant. Keeps you from overeating."

"How long have I been on all these pills?"

"Mrs. Lewis, it doesn't matter," she ignored my question. "Do you want to lay back down?"

"No. I'm going with you and Michaela to gym practice."

Ida's brown eyes shot open wide. "You *are*?"

"Why wouldn't I? She's my daughter." Quite frankly, gymnastics was one of the things I missed out on, having two kids who adored football and basketball.

"Well…if you insist. Fine. But be sure to take your medication first."

"I don't need any medication, Ida. I feel great."

She took a long drag of air. "I'll have to ask Mr. Lewis, then. He doesn't want any more...public incidents."

"Public incidents my foot," I told her, springing from the bed. "What time do we leave?"

Chapter 5

I nearly got lost in my closet trying to find something to wear to gymnastics practice. Didn't make any sense how many clothes and shoes I'd racked up in that closet. Everything slipped on as though it has been fitted for to my body. Imagine my surprise to find that was exactly the case. I found the tailor's card tacked to the wall.

No wonder I have to stay this size—I wouldn't be able to wear anything otherwise.

If Ida had reservations about me going earlier, she certainly didn't know what to think of me as I walked through the house taking pictures on my cell phone. Exquisite paintings, a spiral staircase, a chandelier that danced with a million lights.

"This house is beautiful!" I gasped as Ida, Michaela, and I traveled down a scraped hardwood hallway. "Who decorated it?"

Ida stopped. She turned sharply, landed me right in her face. "Mrs. Lewis, are you sure you don't want to take your medicine?"

"Yes. I'm sure."

"You seem awfully, forgetful. I could ask Dr. Roundhouse for something to help you with your memory," she suggested.

"I appreciate your concern for me, but Dr. Roundhouse is the one who needs to be on something if he's prescribing drugs every time somebody experiences a bad mood," I exclaimed.

She huffed. "Dr. Roundhouse is a woman. Which proves my point."

"Dr. Roundhouse is a nut. Let's go."

Ida's eyes widened. She turned on her heels and marched onward.

Michaela giggled. I smiled at her and took her hand. We sped up to keep pace with Ida.

A brisk winter wind met us in the porte-cochere, where a sleek, black Lincoln town car was waiting for us. Ida opened the back door from the passenger's side. Michaela bounded inside.

I opened the front door.

"Are you sure you want to sit in the front?" Ida questioned. "The sunlight. Your eyes."

What about my eyes?

"Come sit with me, Mommy," Michaela called as she patted the empty space next to her.

"Okay."

Given the children's coldness earlier, I would gladly sit next to my daughter.

Once we were all buckled up, Ida backed out of the side driveway and I was able to see my house for the first time. "Wow! Three floors!" The Mediterranean style boasted stone accents and classic red tiles. From the looks of the outside, I hadn't seen half my house. And there was another house behind the pool! *Nice.*

Ida's phone rang. She answered it, using her free hand to keep control of the steering wheel.

"Yes. Yes. I understand, but she insisted…that's correct, Mr. Lewis. It won't happen again."

"Is that my husband?" I yelled to her.

She ignored me.

I tapped her shoulder. "Hey. Ida. Is that Dante on the phone?"

She rolled her eyes. "Yes."

What's wrong with this chick? "Let me talk to him." I wondered if he sounded anything like Byron.

"He says he'll call you on your phone later," she relayed.

What does he have to discuss with Miss Ida that he cannot discuss with me?

I busied myself talking to Michaela. Once she opened up, I couldn't get her to keep quiet. "Friday, for the Christmas party at school, I'm giving everyone a stamp packet so we can all put stamps on our own papers," she informed me.

"That's awesome, honey."

"And we get out of school early. Miss Bidel said since we have to eat lunch when it's almost breakfast time, we're having breakfast food for lunch." This just tickled her pink.

She went on to ask for a puppy, a reindeer, and then she wanted to know if she could sleep in the media room Friday night.

Ida butted into our conversation, "No, Michaela. Your father will be home tomorrow."

"I say yes," I overrode the woman who had obviously put herself in the front seat of this car as well as my life. "Let's sleep in the media room Friday night. Me, you, DJ, and Daddy."

"Really, Mommy?" she squealed.

"Most definitely."

Ida's brown hair shook back and forth as she glared at me through the rearview mirror.

I kissed Michaela on the forehead. "I have a secret to tell you." I cupped my hand over her ear. "I look forward to our adventure."

She imitated my gesture. I bent down so that she could give me her secret message. "I love you."

I pinched her brown cheeks. "I love you, too."

I couldn't have asked for more adorable kids in my dreams.

Miss Ida was the one who needed to learn to relax, not me. She followed me around the gymnasium as though I might break an expensive vase.

"Ida, this is not necessary" I finally told her as I walked out of the women's restroom and found her standing near the entrance, obviously waiting on me. "I am a grown woman. I don't need you to supervise me."

She licked her dry lips. "Yes, I do. It's part of my job."

I transferred my weight to one hip. "Could you please remind me, what exactly is your job description?"

Her chest heaved with laughter. "I'm the Nanny, I'm your assistant, I manage the household." She bobbed her head up and down. "I'm pretty much…"

"The woman of the house," I completed her sentence.

She stuck her hands in her pocket and gave me a sheepish grin. "Yeah. I guess so."

Well, if she's the woman of the house, what am I? With an estate as large as ours, I certainly needed help. But this woman was also running my family.

"Do you ever go home?"

"Of course, I go home, Mrs. Lewis. I live in the guest house."

I could tell my questions were confusing her again. "I don't mean home to my guest house. I mean, *home* home. To *your* family."

"My family is in England, remember?"

"Oh, yeah. I forgot."

Now that I was talking to her woman-to-woman, I recognized myself in Ida. She was so busy taking care of everyone else, but didn't have a life of her own. *Is this my fault?*

We walked back to the parent seating area. I wanted to ask more questions, but I didn't want to heighten Ida's suspicions.

I focused on Michaela for the rest of the practice. She twirled and waved at me. She flipped and winked at me. Every ounce of her was glad to have me at practice with the other moms whose presence alone gave encouragement.

Michaela was pooped after practice. I picked her up and carried her back into the house. She wrapped her arms around my neck and thanked me.

"Okay, Michaela. Let's get down and go take a bath," Ida told my daughter.

"It's all right, Ida. I'll give her the bath tonight."

Michaela squeezed tighter.

Ida raised her eyebrows for what must have been the fiftieth time that evening. "As you wish, Mrs. Lewis."

"Call me Chaka, okay?"

"No, Mrs. Lewis. I can't—".

"Yes, you can. Say it with me. Cha-ka."

She hesitated. "Chaaaa—"

"Ka!" I completed.

"Chaka," she finally said.

She left Michaela and I to ourselves, which gave me great relief until I realized I had no idea where Michaela was supposed to bathe.

"Michaela, let's play a game."

Though sleepy, she raised her head. "What's it called?"

"It's called…name that room," I invented right on the spot.

She giggled and clapped twice. "Yaay! How do we play?"

"First, you have to get on my back." Without her feet touching the ground, we managed to get her in position. "Now, we're going to walk *all* through the house. And when we come to a room, you'll whisper in my ear and tell me what every room is for. Like if I were a stranger."

"Mommy, you're so silly today," she laughed. "I like playing with you."

With Michaela as my guide, I toured the mansion, taking note of its layout. The structure was shaped like a giant, three-story "U". I counted six bedrooms and 7.5 bathrooms. Three living areas, two offices, a media room, a library, a laundry room, a craft room, and an exercise room filled with the latest equipment to keep my husband's body in shape.

And might I add, Dante Lewis was in excellent shape. His muscles glistened on an oversized, framed cover of ESPN magazine. Deep brown skin, a six-pack, ripped arms. He had a boyish face that contrasted the manly muscles. It was easy to see why I had fallen in love with him.

The 10-foot tall Christmas tree in the living room was filled with expertly placed decorations. Nothing from the kids, no string of homemade popcorn. The mounds of presents underneath showed no trace of the kids having wrapped anything for my parents or their cousins. It was all too perfect, really.

We found DJ alone in his room playing video games. I suppose with boys, some things don't change.

"Hi, DJ," I interrupted him.

His eyes stayed glued to the screen.

"Hey, DJ. Mommy said we could watch movies all night tomorrow night in the theater room!"

He paused the game. Looked up at us. "Did Daddy say?"

"Well, no, but I think it's a good idea. Don't you?" I nodded.

He resumed his imaginary battle. "Daddy and Miss Ida won't allow us."

I wanted to tell DJ that Miss Ida was not his mother, and his father and I were perfectly capable of spending quality time with him. I didn't want to disrupt things too much.

"DJ is a sourpuss," Michaela whispered in my ear.

I busted out laughing so hard I almost dropped her. "Michaela, you are too much."

After baths and dinner, I read the kids a bedtime story. Ida must have checked on me six times that evening. "Is everything okay?" "Do you need anything?" I wanted to shoo her away. However, her third time through, it occurred to me that she loved my children and had been raising them for most of their lives. It was heartless of me to suddenly shut her out.

"Could you help Michaela with her hair?" I gave Ida a place.

After we put the children to bed, Ida popped up at my bedroom door again. "Come in."

She walked softly toward me as I was wrapping my hair in a silk scarf. "I don't know what came over you today, but you weren't yourself. Dr. Roundhouse has ordered me to make sure you take the correct dose of sleeping pills tonight."

I slapped a spot on the bed. "Ida, come. Sit down."

She obeyed.

I tied the scarf twice. "I'm not taking those pills tonight."

She exhaled loudly. "Are you trying to have me fired? If you want a new assistant, why don't you just say so? I'll oversee the search committee for my replacement." Tears pooled under her blue eyes.

"Ida, I don't have a problem with you. All I'm saying—and you said it yourself—is that I'm not the same as I used to be. I'm better now. I don't want to take those pills anymore."

"You need them, Mrs. Le—"

"Chaka."

"You need them, *Chaka*," she pleaded with me.

"No, I don't. Maybe I used to. Maybe life was really, really overwhelming for me at one point and I needed meds. But I'm perfectly capable of handling life without pharmaceutical assistance from this day forward. I appreciate everything you've done to watch out for me. I appreciate Dr. Roundhouse for doing whatever it is she's done to help me cope. But I am okay now. Capiche?"

She slapped both hands on her thighs and stood. "If you say so, Chaka. I'll assess you in the morning. Don't forget, you've got to be up at six for your workout with Jabari. And taping for the show starts at ten."

"The show?"

"Yes, the show."

I gave a nervous laugh. "Right. The show." I gave her two thumbs-up. "I gotcha."

No sooner than she excused herself, I grabbed my phone, this time to research myself. *Chaka Lewis.* 2,175,000 results. *Seriously?*

There were pictures of me, videos of me, mostly tied to the first few episodes of a new reality show— *NFL Wives of Dallas!*

In that instant, I knew I had to be dreaming. *I'm becoming a celebrity!* Soon, people all over the world would *know* me!

No more dead-end jobs! No more disrespectful bosses! Granted, I would miss Byron. He certainly wasn't missing me, though. *Married to Tya Longfield!* My heart still ached for Corey and London, and yet I had already been won over by Michaela. DJ would take a little more effort.

Forget all that. *I'm a celebrity! I have a life!*

I hardly slept, thinking about the taping. Jabari, a twenty-something-year-old hunk, had no sympathy for my droopy eyes or the fact that it was five o'clock in the morning and the sun hadn't even considered rising yet.

He met me in front of the house. "Let's get warmed up. Two miles."

Two miles!

He took off jogging. I promise you, the only thing that kept me going was an occasional glance at his behind in front of me. *Is my husband's behind that fine?* I guesstimated I'd make it a tenth of a mile before conking out, but I was wrong. This new body of mine could hang.

My lungs, my legs, my arms all worked in unison like a well-oiled machine. I even had enough breath to carry a light conversation with Jabari as we jogged. *I got this.*

Oh, I spoke too soon. Jabari would not leave well enough alone. We circled back to the house, where the real torture took place. Squats, lifting weights, some kind of blow-up-balancing ball that made me squeeze my stomach so hard, I wondered if I'd be able to eat breakfast.

We finished the workout with stretching.

"Good job, Mrs. Lewis."

"Thanks," I panted as my body cooled down.

"So. Ida tells me you have decided to stop taking your pills," he stated.

"Why is Ida talking to you about my pills?" I grumbled.

"I'm your personal trainer. It's my job to know what's happening with your body."

Made sense. "She's right. I've stopped."

He leaned over at the waist and grabbed his toes. "Did you consult with Dr. Roundhouse?"

I touched my toes as well. "I'm sure Ida's already given you the answer to that question."

"Touché. I'll admit you are much sharper this morning."

"Thank you."

"You think Dante's gonna like the new-attitude you?"

I stood erect. "Why wouldn't he?"

Jabari smirked. "I'm just asking."

We got down on the ground, on mats, for what turned out to be back-popping stretches, Yoga, or something of the likes.

"Jabari, can I ask you a question?"

"Shoot."

"What do you think of Dante? *Really*?"

His lips were preparing to speak what I hoped would be the truth. Then he cleared his throat. "I think he signs my checks."

Should have known. "I see."

Chapter 6

Ida dropped me off at the studio office and, immediately, a swarm of show assistants surrounded me.

"Would you like some water, Chaka?" "You look marvelous!" A girl could get used to this. From my left, a flash of light.

"Get them out of here!" a woman screamed.

Paparazzi! Taking my picture! I hoped I had picked the right outfit, curled my hair just so, and applied my makeup in a way that wouldn't land me on a magazine cover showing the world what *not* to do.

The show assistants whisked me into a grand, hotel-ish building with an abstract sculpture taking center stage, pointing toward the skylight high above the ground floor. In this place, everyone was beautiful. Platform heels, short skirts, men in skinny jeans.

I followed a young lady who seemed to be my leader, up the elevator and down the hallway to a large conference room. I recognized two of the women from my Internet search. Tonya Hall and Xandria Tolbert, both married to my husband's teammates.

"Hello, Chaka! So good to see you again!" Tonya stood and hugged me.

Totally fake.

"Good to see you, as well, love."

Pot calling the kettle black.

Due to spacing, it would have been hard for me to make it around to the other ladies, so I greeted them from across the table.

Looking at my show-mates made me realize that working out with Jabari wasn't simply a matter of health. If I developed a roll of fat, I couldn't live in this space. Be with these people at this level. One piece of Momma's pound cake could put me in jeopardy.

No wonder I'm so anxious all the time. My genes weren't made for this.

In walked three men—one wearing a suit and two others who were so underdressed for this professional meeting that they must have been creative geniuses.

"Welcome, everyone. Let's go over today's plan," one of the artsy ones commanded. "Today, we're taping the fight between Chaka and Xandria."

"Let's get it on!" Xandria smiled at me.

Wait? We're having a fight and we know ahead of time?

The second artist turned to me and spoke in classic male-hairdresser mode, "Chaka, this is a really, really big episode. You have got to work it like a first class witch, with a B. You hear me, girlfriend?"

The disappointment must have shown on my face. He fanned his hand toward me and said, "Don't worry. We'll save your reputation by the fourth show. But for now, you're the villain on the show. The blogs and tweets will be blowin' you up, honey, hashtag N-F-L Wives Chaka!"

The man in the black suit didn't say anything. He listened, nodded. No facial expression.

"So, Pat, are we still shooting at Francesca's house?" Xandria asked the first man.

"Yes. As I mentioned last week, your main argument will take place at the indoor pool. That's where we'll have the fight, and Chaka will push you into the highly chlorinated pool water wearing the mink coat Calloway just bought you."

"What are we arguing about?" I wanted to know, still flabbergasted that we were planning a fight! Felt like Junior High School, when we used to meet up at the bus stop to pass a few licks.

"Good question," the second man spoke again. "Who's got something?"

Within a matter of minutes, my fellow housewives and the artistic directors concocted the foulest, most unladylike conversations that would escalate to me pushing Xandria into Francesca's swimming pool. Afterward, I was stomp out of her house, escorted by rent-a-cops. All the while, we'd be cussing screaming, and threatening each other. Over nothing.

"Now, Chaka, when you and Xandria start fighting, she's going to get the best of you. Wardrobe's going to put you in something low-cut so we can stage Xandria ripping at your chest." He pre-enacted the scene, clawing at his own shirt. "We're going to blur out your entire chest area to make it seem as though your boobs completely popped out during the fight!"

"Brilliant!" Tonya screamed. "You have *got* to show this scene on the previews."

Wait a minute! I don't want my plastic boobs pretend-blurred out! What if Michaela sees this show?

"Let's do it!" Pat declared.

Everyone rose from the table. I followed the ladies to the dressing room, where a team of stylists erased my attempts at beautifying myself and turned it up ten notches.

An hour later, my hair and makeup were on point. And I was wearing a V-neck sweater that barely covered my girls.

Needless to say, none of this fit my personal style. If I was going to fight someone, I wanted to get really mad and mean it.

We taped and cut, taped and cut for an hour at least. Frustration started to set in because Tonya kept messing up. All she had to do was come in, sit her size two behind down, and ask Xandria about her coat.

As Xandria, Francesca, another woman named Elizabeth, and I waited for the directors to reiterate Tonya's simple role, Elizabeth made the comment that Francesca needed to turn on the heat because it was freezing in their house.

To which Xandria added. "For real. Y'all forget to pay the light bill?"

My teeth were chattering so hard, I could barely laugh. "I know, right?"

Francesca didn't take the joke lightly. "Don't start with me."

"I'm just saying, it is cold in here," from Elizabeth. "You'd think if you were gonna have an indoor pool, you would make sure it was properly insulated."

The camera crew inched toward us and it was *on*.

"I didn't invite you here to begin with," Francesca bit back.

Oh my gosh, we never made it to my fight with Xandria because Francesca and Elizabeth got into it for real. Kinda sorta. I mean, it was cold and Francesca did need to turn up the heat. But it wasn't that serious.

Maybe they had some kind of real beef brewing that I wasn't privy to. All I know is, the cameras kept rolling, Pat was jumping up and down on the sidelines with excitement, Elizabeth pushed Xandria in the pool, and on Xandria's way down, she seized my shirt. My breast popped out *for real* and everyone gasped in disbelief.

Next thing I know, I'm submerged in this ice cold water.

Xandria and I came up gasping for air. I swear, I could have punched her in the face! This was *not* part of the plan. All the staged curse words I'd been mentally practicing came bubbling out of me as I dog-paddled to stay afloat. She gracefully stroked to the edge of the pool and got out.

My limbs began to stiffen. The water was so cold. "Help!" The cameras kept rolling as my chin dip below the surface. "Help me!"

Francesca yelled to me, "All you have to do is stand up!"

I stretched out my legs to test her theory. It worked. I stood up in the four-foot pool and the entire set erupted in laughter.

"T*hat* is what we call priceless footage!" Elizabeth hooted.

"Absolutely part of the previews!" Pat agreed.

Excellent. Now I'm the stupid one on the show.

Following my reality show fiasco, I didn't feel much like sleeping in the media room. Michaela was so pumped and excited, however. I couldn't let her down. Ida helped us with the popcorn and drinks. All the while, she kept telling me this wasn't a good idea. Dante wouldn't be happy.

I assured her that I could handle Dante, and I had every reason to think I could. My hair was back in full commission. Makeup perfect. Honestly, I was excited about seeing my sexy husband for the first time.

At around seven, I gave Ida leave for the evening. "Enjoy a night to yourself, for once."

"Thank you." She cupped my hands into hers and squeezed. "Please. Call me if you need *anything* tonight. Anything at all."

"Sure will."

The kids and I sat on the middle row of the theater. For the first twenty minutes of the movie, DJ kept turning around, checking the door.

"Son, just enjoy the show," I calmed him. "Here. Have some popcorn."

Another half-hour later, the three of us were lost in the movie when suddenly, the overhead lights flashed on us.

There stood my husband. *Good God Almighty.* He was ten times more attractive in person, except for the ugly snarled-up expression on his face. "What the—"

"Hi, honey!" I intercepted him with a smile. "It's so good to have you home."

I climbed over Michaela and ran to my man. I tried to throw my arms around him, but he ducked me completely and swerved to the left. "DJ. What are y'all doing in here?"

I recovered in time to see my son's eyes fill with utter terror. "Um, mom said we—"

"Get out!" Dante raged.

In haste, Michaela accidentally spilled the half-full bowl of popcorn on the floor. "Oh no!" she cried.

"Clean it up!" my husband hissed. His jaw muscles tightened.

I rushed to help the kids clean up the mess. "It was an accident."

"It shouldn't have happened. Not in *here*! And you'd better get every drop of it."

Perhaps I could have chalked his nasty mood up to the fact that the Cowboys had gotten blown-out the night before. But when he mumbled, "Stupid!" under his breath, something crawled all the way up my spine and back down to my gut.

"Michaela and DJ, go on to bed. We'll watch a movie tomorrow night. Mommy will finish cleaning it up." I needed a word with Mr. Dante Lewis one-on-one.

The kids scrambled off the row and up the steps, two at a time. Only DJ stopped on his way out. His eyes wide as when he'd first seen me, he asked, "Momma, do you want me to call Miss Ida?"

"No."

"You sure?"

Why would I need Miss Ida? "Yes, I'm sure. Toodles."

With the children out of the room, I put my hand on my hip and let my backbone slip. "What is your problem, Mister?"

Dante unzipped his backpack. He dug out a DVD, threw the backpack on one of the empty chairs. "Chaka, I know you've been off your medication, but don't let that be the reason for you to act crazy as you want to tonight."

"What's *crazy* is you rolling up in here scaring our kids half to death and calling them stupid!"

"Stupid is as stupid does," he quoted Forrest Gump.

I crossed my arms and watched as he walked to the right of the big screen, opened the glass cabinet door to the control center, and inserted the DVD.

"You know, yesterday and today, I watched videos of you online. Talking about how important it is to work as a team, the value of being patient your teammates, building each other up. But then you come home and tear down your own kids?"

"Chaka, you need to go to take your freakin' pills and go to bed." He kept his eyes on the screen.

"And what's with all these pills? Don't you know if I'm talking uppers *and* downers, there's something seriously wrong with me? Why would you keep drugging me? You want a zombie for a wife?"

He inhaled. Exhaled.

Behind me, the screen filled with an image of players on football field. Xs and Os with arrows and lines. He was either studying the last game or preparing for the next one.

"Are you listening to me?"

He raised both eyebrows, refusing eye contact. "This is my last time telling you to leave me alone."

"And this is *my* last time asking you for an explanation for why find it necessary to be so mean to the kids?" I stood my ground about six feet from him.

When I say that man was in my face in less than a second, I am not exaggerating. He hit my body with his shoulders and threw me—I mean, picked me up and threw me!—against the wall. "I said get out!"

My back hit hard and I slid down to a heap on the floor. I wouldn't have believed it I hadn't been there myself. *This man is crazy.*

"Get up!" He kicked my hip and I tumbled to one side. He picked me up and literally stood me on my feet. "And get out."

I limped back up the steps and into the hallway with him following right behind me. He slammed the door too soon, sending me hurling across the path, into the opposite wall.

Again, I landed on the floor.

My God! What just happened to me? All of a sudden, my beautiful surroundings meant absolutely nothing to me. The elegant décor, the crown molding, the custom lighting, all of it was like spraying perfume on a skunk.

I lay on the floor, still trying to make sense of things, and began to cry into the contemporary, patterned carpet. Out of the corner of my eye, I saw something move just beyond the bathroom door.

"Who's there?"

Slowly, DJ crawled toward me. He rubbed my top-of-the-line weave. "It's okay, Mommy. Everything will be fine."

"Is your Daddy *always* like this?"

He shook his head. "Not always."

"Sweetheart, how many times have you seen him hit me?"

My heart broke as he tried to count on his fingers.

"Never mind," I stopped him. "Has he hit you?"

He didn't answer. *My baby.*

DJ hooked his elbow onto mine. "Come to bed and take your pills. You'll feel better tomorrow."

My son could hardly carry my weight, yet every single ounce of support he offered eased the throbbing pains shooting through my entire backside. I promise, Dante hit me like he was trying to stop me at fourth and inches.

DJ helped me into bed. He tucked me in as best as she could, then opened the medicine drawer. He took the empty glass on my nightstand to the restroom and filled it with water. Carefully, he set it down again.

Clearly, my son had done this before.

"I'm not taking the medication. You go ahead and get back to your room before Daddy catches you in here."

He skirted away.

I clutched my phone in hand, unlocked it with my thumbprint, and dialed 9-1-1.

The police arrived with minutes. They interviewed me. Interviewed the children, who must have been too afraid to tell the truth. My husband showed them the six bottles of mind-altering medication I had been prescribed.

The cops left within the hour. No arrest was made, only a promise for box seats at the next game.

Dante stood our bedroom doorway. "Don't you *ever* pull that crap again."

He left me alone.

I cried long, trembling sobs afterward. *God, my life is a nightmare. Please help me.*

No soothing scriptures came to mind.

I missed my husband, Byron, terribly. For all I knew, he could have been cuddled up with Tya.

My sons. At the same time, how could I miss my old family while DJ and Michaela were suffering?

Though I had only known these children for a matter of days, both families were so real. Different dynamics, but very real, at least in my head. Did it matter that I remembered more about one family than another?

How did I get here? Maybe I really am crazy?

The anxiety sweeping through my brain threatened to cut my breath short.

In desperation I reached for the sleeping pills. The glass of water. The bottle said to take one. If memory served me well, I could take two and sleep longer.

I placed both pills on my tongue and swallowed them with water.

Now I knew why I needed them.

I closed my eyes and drifted off into the deepest sleep I had never known.

Chapter 7

Bleep. Bleep. Bleep.

Blackness.

"She's on a lot of medication, baby." The voice of my mother.

I tell her to take Michaela and DJ away from Dante. But the words I say in my head won't come out of my mouth.

"When will she wake up?" A child's voice. Not Michaela or DJ.

"We don't know." Her words crack slightly.

"Keep praying for her, London."

London!

Chapter 8

"Chaka," a vaguely familiar voice called my name. My eyelids, however, felt like 5-pound weights.

A strong hand shook my body. "Chaka. Get up."

My mouth was too dry to form words. *Those sleeping pills don't play.* I moaned to acknowledge whoever was attempting to interrupt my much-needed sleep.

The idea that Dante might be the person on the other end of that arm pushed me to get beyond the drowsiness. His temper had already begun to dictate my behavior.

I forced my eyelids open. My ivory and silver surroundings were gone, replaced by what I would consider a "normal" bedroom, only it wasn't mine.

"Chaka!" The man yelled this time as he kneeled on the bed beside me, looking into my eyes with concern.

Oh. My. God. "Calvin?"

"Girl, you had me going there for a minute. Come on, let's get up. We're running late." He kissed me on my forehead before hopping away toward what I presumed was a master bathroom because the next thing I heard coming from that direction was a shower.

My soul flooded with a giddiness I hadn't known since he and I were in love, back in the day. Yes, I loved Byron. But *Calvin* was different. I felt sixteen again, full of endless possibilities.

I'm married to Calvin Rippley! Wait a minute. Or maybe I'm still married to Byron, but I'm cheating on him with Calvin. I couldn't say the thought had never crossed my mind.

Quickly, I examined my left hand. A solitaire rested on my ring finger next to a plain band. This was not the ring that signified my union with Byron.

Calvin actually married me?

A fresh wave of energy flowed through me as I rose up to stretch myself and take in my surroundings. Mahogany wood for the headboard and footboard. A large mosaic rug covering ceramic tile. Two identical dressers, both with mirrors on top. An entertainment center with a television. Nothing outside of the ordinary purchases one might make at Lowes or J.C. Penney. We weren't rich, but we were proud because somebody was certainly keeping this room neat.

The most prominent fixtures in our bedroom were three bookshelves, which took up an entire wall, full of novels. I counted thirty-seven on one row. There were five shelves in each case. Multiply that number by three and I began to suspect that I might have a little novel-fetish going on.

Is this real? I pinched myself, like people said, to check. I hadn't done that when I was married to Dante. Maybe that proved Dante wasn't totally real. This marriage to Calvin, however, could definitely be real. We went way back, before I ever even met Byron. I had loved Calvin so long it made sense that, finally, we were together.

My knee scraped against something in the bed. I reached under the covers, and there it was again. My diary.

This Diary belongs to Chaka Rippley. If found, please keep your nosey eyes out of it. Just call me: 214-555-8721.

I certainly was bolder than I could remember.

October 20

Dear Me,

I need a little more Jesus because Sandra is about to make me go all the way left. I'm so mad, I can't even write about it right now. If Calvin doesn't do something soon, I may end up in jail.

-Chaka

Whoever Sandra was, I needed to stay away from her.

Thanksgiving Day-

Today was so sad. I miss my father so much. Still can't believe he's gone sometimes. It's like a bad dream that won't end. Calvin knows how hard this time of year is on me. He was so sweet to me today. I love me some him.

-Chaka

"Awwww," I cooed. How nice to have a wonderful, thoughtful husband for once.

December 14

Went shopping today. Ran into you-know-how. I wish Sandra could be out of my life forever!!! Not dead. Just POOF, be GONE. She is an entire rosebush's worth of thorns in my side, for real. Why, God?

Calvin and I had our date night last night. Movie and dinner. Dessert at home. Huge smile on my face this morning ☺ Sometimes I think it's not healthy for me to love someone so much. Can't help it, though.

I should start a blog about good husbands because I see so many people online talking about how awful theirs are.

I just wish he could see Sandra for who she is.

Keeping a blog would make me write more, something I need to do anyway.

Maybe.

-Chaka

I was going to have to find my old journals to figure out this Sandra chick. Maybe it was time for me and Sandra's relationship to come to an end.

Additionally, I wanted to discover exactly how and when Calvin came back in the picture because I certainly wanted to read that love story.

"Chaka, did you hear me? We gotta get moving or we'll be late for Sierra's game," Calvin rushed me again. He always was a stickler for time.

"Okay. I'm coming." Unsure of exactly what I was supposed to be doing, I figured the first thing I would do in the morning no matter who I was married to would be to brush my teeth.

I followed Calvin's cheerful hum to the restroom. Brushing my teeth gave me the excuse I needed to stand in one place and study Calvin as he shaved.

Just as handsome as I remembered him. Five foot ten, light brown skin, wavy hair as a result of his bi-racial heritage. All the girls used to pass notes about how good he looked, and he took full advantage of their admiring glances. Calvin had an on-and-off girlfriend, the infinitely popular Alexis Hunter, back then. But he was a playboy who (I heard) roamed the field every time they broke up.

And now he's all mine.

"Show you a few thangs…show you a few thangs," he crooned. I knew the popular Justin Timberlake song. I also knew the woman in the mirror well.

Not much had changed about my appearance. Pudgy stomach, the outline of the double chin to come. If I could get in touch with Jabari—and afford him—I would definitely utilize his services again because my body was slammin' when I was married to Dante. *If* I was ever married to Dante.

How are Michaela and DJ? Ida?

"Dang, baby, you tryin' to scrape the enamel off your teeth?" he laughed.

I leaned over the sink and spat. After rinsing the sink and my toothbrush, I washed my face. Calvin was almost finished shaving. When he stopped to wipe his face, I gave him the hug I'd wanted to give him for as long as I could remember.

"Good morning to you, too." He hugged me back.

I kissed his chest, planted my head on his heart.

"Look here, don't start nothin' we can't finish this morning. The game starts in less than an hour." He released me and walked straight to the closet.

The mere mention of intimacy with Calvin put my stomach on a rollercoaster. I'd never slept with anyone other than Byron. Would it be…different with somebody else? Better? Worse?

Calvin flew out of the restroom. I trailed him to the walk-in closet and watched his selection of clothing to determine mine. He grabbed a hoodie, a pair of jeans, and a distinctive pair of suede lace-up shoes, styled like bowling shoes.

On my side, I found a pair of black corduroys and a thick blue sweater. A pair of Nikes completed my outfit.

When I walked out of the closet, there was Calvin standing in front of a full-length mirror. Wearing his birthday suit.

I stepped back into the closet, covering my eyes. "I'm sorry."

"Sorry for what?"

My system was in shock. Aside from a few magazines passed around in the dorm, I had never seen another man's private parts in person. I had also never seen a man with so much…boobage.

Should I be thinking about this?

I dropped my eyes to the floor as I emerged from the closet again and dressed.

Calvin made up the bed, and we were off to some sporting event. I wanted to ask where this "Sierra" child was, but I couldn't do so without giving myself away. I figured maybe she'd spent the night with a teammate or he'd taken her to meet with the team earlier in the morning, while I was still knocked out.

Didn't matter to me, though. I liked having Calvin to myself. We talked and laughed all the way there about the Real Housewives of Atlanta and Miami. Then he asked me if I'd replayed the one he recorded for me about the Dallas NFL wives.

"No, I didn't…see it in the recordings."

"You have to watch it. It's going to be a good show," he recommended.

"Is Dante Lewis's wife in the cast?"

He looked me upside my head. "Babe, what you know about the Cowboys?"

"Nothing. I'm just asking," I lied.

"Yeah, she's on there. She seems weird. Like she's on drugs. Something's wrong with her," he predicted.

"Mmmm." *If only you knew.*

I stared out the window, watching two kids on their bicycles ride down the sidewalk a few blocks from our house. I knew this area of Dallas well. Middle-class hard-working people who always seemed a step above Byron and I. Reports said most of the middle class was only two paychecks away from homelessness. Byron and I had only been *one* paycheck away from apartmentlessness.

Calvin's Hummer H3 couldn't compete with the multitude of vehicles Dante had in the garage, but there was a certain sense of security in knowing that whenever Calvin had given some thought to buying a vehicle, he hadn't started off thinking about the cheapest thing on the lot.

I could live this life forever.

Walking into the football stadium with Calvin felt like walking down a high school hallway with him. Women— *grown women!*—smiled at him while completely ignoring me. Being his natural cordial self, Calvin smiled back. Tilted his chin and said 'hello.'

I could have sworn he initiated the friendly-woman hellos a time or two himself.

I was a long way from my insecure days as a 13-year-old, scrawny-legged toothpick, but these women were taking me back down memory lane. Was I good enough? Cute enough to be with Calvin? I'd always had a hard time reconciling a really nice-looking man with an average-looking woman.

When I was married to Dante, we made a handsome couple.

Stop the presses! I'm not ugly! Even if I were, I believe Calvin would still love me. Get ahold of yourself, Chaka!

Calvin found seats halfway up the stands on the forty-yard line. He opened my portable cushioned seat for me and waited for me to get comfortable before he sat on the cold, hard bench.

Such a gentleman. "Thank you."

He began craning his neck, looking at the high school-aged cheerleaders on the sidelines. "I don't see Sierra."

She's old enough to be in high school? That would mean I had her at age fifteen or sixteen. I didn't even start talking to Calvin as a friend until late in our senior year. *This is weird.*

As spectators filled the stands, Calvin seemed to be entranced with people-watching. I followed his line of vision in an effort to determine what he continued to find so interesting. Through careful observation, it seemed to me that Calvin's eyes lingered quite a while on pretty women.

But in my diary, I had said that he was a wonderful husband. Attentive. Caring.

Maybe my eyes were playing tricks on me.

His cell phone rang. "Hello? Yeah. We're at the forty. Walk down this way and look up." He ended the call.

"Who was that?"

"My mother."

Calvin gave a big, country wave, and up came a woman who had definitely given birth to my husband judging by the forehead and mouth. She wore a long, curly frontlace wig and a blinged-out velour pants/jacket combo. This would be my first time actually meeting her—to my recollection, of course.

She politely squeezed past the people on the end of our row. Calvin hugged her. They both sat down. I leaned forward. "Hello!"

She rolled her eyes my way. "Hello."

What's her deal?

"There she is!" Calvin toward the cheerleaders, whipping out his cell phone.

"I can't see that far. Which one is Sierra?" my mother-in-law asked, thankfully.

"With the pink bow."

"Oh! I see her!"

According to the pre-game announcements, it was "little sister" spirit night at our local high school. Sierra and a bunch of other pre-teen girls who looked to be the same age as London were performing with the varsity squad.

"As I call their names, would the families of our special guests please stand. Kindall Deeves."

The way her family hoora'd, sounded like graduation. Six names later it was our turn. "Sierra Riddley."

"Woop! Woop! Woop!" Calvin chanted, pumping his fists.

"Yaay! Go Sierra!" my mother in-law shouted. "That's my grandbaby!"

Not to be outdone, I hollered, "Great job, Sierra! Mommy loves you!"

At which point, my husband and his mother stopped their cheering and looked at me like I had grown a second head.

"I…I *do* love her," I stood up for myself. *What kind of mother am I?*

The announcer called the next little girl's name. Our crew sat back down.

My stomach coiled into knots as I wondered what I had done wrong.

"I'll go get us some snacks," Calvin offered.

"Okay," I said.

My husband was barely two steps away before my mother-in-law tore into me. "Don't you ever try to confuse Sierra like that again!"

"I'm not—"

"Then quit tryin' to force your way in. Sierra's already got a mother, and a darn good one, too!"

I held my breath. *I'm not Sierra's mother?* "I am so sorry."

She nodded, faced the field again. "You got *that* much right."

Chapter 9

Thanks to a few of our church members who had come to the game, I figured out that "Sandra" was Calvin's mother, which must have been the reason he sat between us the whole time.

I knew from reading the diaries that I couldn't stand her. She was rude and bossy to me all evening. Yet, she could be as sweet as pie to Calvin and the church folk. She obviously had something against me and I was determined to pull it out of Calvin because I couldn't go through the rest of my marriage hating my mother-in-law.

One good thing I could say about Byron's family was that they accepted me wholeheartedly. Sometimes, they felt more like my family than his.

But I'm not married to Byron anymore.

This whole thing was still so unbelievable. If I went too many more days with these untraceable memories in my brain, I might need counseling to silence my vivid imagination.

Sierra rode back home with us in order to spend the night. She and Calvin caught up the whole way. She was smart as a whip, and I could tell she had her Daddy wrapped around her finger. Their relationship was cute.

She barely had two words for me, though. I attempted to join the conversation at natural breaks, but neither Calvin nor my stepdaughter seemed to want to include me. I settled for eavesdropping, which provided several clues. She was in the fifth grade. Her birthday was coming up on New Year's Day, and her mother was a teacher.

When we got home, Calvin spent the next half hour with Sierra, leaving me to myself. I used the time to take the grand tour. Three bedrooms, two and a half baths. Two living areas and an office. Back in our bedroom, I found a cell phone on a charger. I touched the screen and professionally photographed picture of Calvin and I appeared. *Must be mine.*

Curiosity forced me to enter "Byron Stringer" into the search window. He was listed as a coach on a little league football team, which didn't surprise me one bit. I found pictures of him with a little boy. For some reason, I searched for Corey and London, too. No useful hits.

My husband stood at the doorway of our bedroom. "Hey, Sierra and I are going to the movies."

"Sounds great! I'll get my coat since I'm always cold—"

"Me and her," he reiterated.

My shoulders slumped. "Can I tag along?"

She sucked in air between his teeth. "Chaka, it's still too soon."

Too soon for what? "Fine. If you say so."

He entered the room and joined me on the bed. "Baby, don't be upset. Please? Why don't you just, you know, read a book?" He motioned toward my bookcases. "Or go by your mom's house."

With those big brown eyes, he could have had anything he wanted out of me. "I'll be fine. You two have a good time."

He kissed my cheek. "You're the best. And you looked beautiful tonight, by the way. We'll be back in a few hours."

My insides warmed with the compliment and his undivided attention, if only for a moment. Calvin certainly charmed his way out of that tight spot.

With the two of them out of the house, I was free to search for my old journals. They weren't in the closet. Not in the back of a drawer. Not in nightstand.

I took a snack break, making myself a sandwich and watching an hour of the news. Should have known all the news stories would revolve around Christmas since we only had two days of shopping left. I realized, then, that I hadn't seen a Christmas tree anywhere in the house. "Where's our tree?" I asked aloud.

The second round of searching for my journals yielded the results I needed. The journals were under my bed, hidden in shoeboxes. I recognized every single one by its exterior. Now that I had time to sit with them, I was able to pinpoint where my entries veered from what I remembered happening: high school graduation day.

From then forward, my relationship with Calvin grew passionate and tumultuous.

June 8
Dear Me,
After graduation, Calvin and I went to the after-parties together. It was like our "coming out" since everyone was used to seeing him with Alexis for so long. Ha! You should have seen the look on her best friend's face! She wanted to scratch my eyes out!
I can't help it if I'm better than Alexis.
-Chaka and Calvin
4-Eva

August 15
Dear Me,

Still can't believe Daddy is making me stay at school all the way until Thanksgiving break before I come home! I miss Calvin like crazy!!! Calvin says he is going to see if he can get a bus ticket to come see me. If he can't, I don't know what I'm going to do.
-Chaka Misses Calvin!

December 8

I'm devastated. Cannot believe this. Would not have imagined this in my wildest dreams. While I've been gone working on my degree, Calvin has been here doing only God knows what with Alexis.
How could he do this to me?
-Chaka will not go down without a fight

The next several entries could have been an episode of a teen drama. Calvin going back and forth between Alexis and I—with a few other girls in the mix, according to rumors passed along to me.

I flipped ahead a few years and cheered for myself when I learned that I had finished college with my English degree. "Yes!" I'd found a job as an editor with an educational publishing company. Calvin was notably absent during those years.

The professional accomplishments were great, but they didn't mean near as much to me as I thought they would. I wanted to get back to the love story.

I found a journal dated around the time Sierra would have been born.

December 28
Dear Me—or whoever I am,
I haven't seen Calvin much lately. Alexis's baby is due any day now. Can hardly breath thinking about this situation. Can't believe it has come to this.
-Chaka

Okay, so the three of us had been in a love triangle and he had cheated on me with Alexis and gotten her pregnant? *Low down, dirty rascal.*

I tried not to get angry, though. We were all young— and it was a long-distance relationship. People get lonely and make mistakes. Calvin and I might not have even been married at the time.

I comforted myself again with the thought that, in the end, *I* was the one wearing the ring. Still, I had to wonder why I loathed Sandra more than Alexis. If anyone should have been my nemesis, Alexis would have been my guess.

The house alarm system beeped. Calvin and Sierra's laughter carried through the house. I listened to their conversation, deciding whether or not to join them in the living room.

I stuffed the journals back into the boxes and tried to wash the residual anger about something that happened almost twelve years ago out of my brain. Apparently, my brain was in a memory-erasing mood already.

I lay back on the bed and switched on the television. An old episode of the *Golden Girls* entertained me while my husband and stepdaughter engaged in noise-talking over video games.

Finally, Calvin entered our room and shed his outer layer of clothing. He climbed on top of me and kissed me tenderly on my lips.

I tried to peck him back, but there were too many questions running through my head at the moment. *Am I married to a cheater? A liar?*

"You good?"

"Yeah," I answered, pushing him off of me.

"What's the matter?"

"I've just been thinking about things."

He sat up on an elbow and stared down into my face.

Man, he's a good listener. I could drown in the amount of attention he gave me.

"Thinking about what?"

"About us. You know…how we got together. Sierra. Alexis," I fished.

Calvin closed his eyes. "Do I need to call Dr. Pace again and set up another counseling appointment?"

We've been to counseling? I had to give him credit for initiating. Obviously, he was willing to work on our relationship. "No, I don't think we need to go again. I just need…closure."

"I thought you *had* closure. All of us had closure. Alexis, too," he tried to help me remember.

"That's good. But what about all the lying and the cheating? I mean…those are deep-down character issues," I said.

He stared at me, perplexed. "We both have to forgive ourselves."

Me?! What did I do wrong?

He continued, "We've both taken complete responsibility for the affair. Alexis has forgiven us. She and I are divorced. You and I are married now, and everyone is moving forward."

I'm a low down dirty, cheatin', lyin', home-wreckin' rascal, too?!

"Really, the only people who still need get over it are Sierra and my mom."

I was ready to sign myself up for Team Sandra because, truly, I was in her corner.

Chapter 10

How could I have ruined a marriage?

Needless to say, I refused to make love to Calvin that night. He stormed out of our bedroom and parked himself on the couch for the night.

I didn't protest because I wanted time alone to finish reading the journals anyway. They sickened me. My suspicions about our love triangle were proven true.

After graduation, Calvin and I started dating, though he never quite ended it completely with Alexis. Next came a series of arguments, busted out car windows, temporary restraining orders, bleached clothes.

I thought I had conquered the world when Calvin and I moved in together. I "beat" Alexis Hunter. But then she "beat" me when they got married. Though it seemed everyone was trying to tell me to let him go, I couldn't. Calvin and I saw each other off and on while he was married to Alexis.

Shortly after Sierra was born, Alexis found enough self-respect to put an end to the foolishness. She divorced him, and I married her rotten leftovers.

I completely disgusted myself. Calvin was wrong, too, of course, but I could only be accountable for Chaka.

We got up early and went to church Sunday morning, still not speaking because I had hurt Calvin's ego by rejecting him. But once our feet hit the parking lot, Calvin was Mr. Congenial, smiling and greeting everyone in the name of the Lord. He even held my hand as we escorted Sierra to children's church. He signed her in, and then continued the façade as we entered the sanctuary.

"Morning, Chaka and Calvin!" the members greeted us in the minutes before the service actually began.

I, for one, had never been inside a church before the service started. *We must be awfully dedicated members.* The choir sang, the preacher preached one of those 'God's gonna turn it around if you put enough money in the offering plate' sermons, service dismissed, and we retrieved Sierra while still smiling and carrying on as though we were the perfect family. Calvin even complimented me when one of the older ladies remarked about how I'd kept my teenage figure.

"That's my love," he bragged with a full smile.

We proceeded back to our car, where the icy cold silent treatment toward me resumed.

"Daddy, can we get some ice cream before you take me back home?"

My maternal instincts kicked in. "It'll spoil your appetite, sweetie. Plus, you don't want to get your pretty dress messy."

Calvin took his eyes off the road long enough to stab me with his eyeballs. "This is an A and B conversation."

My insides absolutely dissolved. I couldn't believe he would treat me so badly, especially in front of Sierra.

"Which store – Braums or Marble Slab?" he overrode me.

Sierra minded her manners by asking me if I wanted anything when they got out of the car to get the ice cream.

"No, honey. Thank you for asking."

This eleven-year-old girl had better sense than my husband.

We arrived at a modest apartment complex. Alexis came out of her unit before Calvin put the car in park. He and Sierra jumped out of the car. She gave her mother a hug. Calvin hugged Alexis, too, and that was when the tears began to flow from my eyes.

Anyone with half a brain and a quarter of a heart could see they still loved each other. It was in the way he pressed into her, the split-second longer she held onto him. Even more painful to observe was the hope twinkling in Sierra's eyes when her parents embraced.

Alexis and Calvin sent Sierra back inside while they stood outside shivering in the cold, talking. I cracked my window to hear what they were saying. Though I couldn't make out their words, the tone of their conversation said this was pleasure, not parent-to-parent business. They were still good friends.

They hugged again. Calvin returned to our car, bouncing up and down in his seat to make body heat. He swished his hands directly in front of the vents to warm them.

He noticed me staring at him. "What?"

"You still love her, don't you?" I sniffed.

The angry exterior he'd donned all morning slipped away. He sighed. "Chaka, we've been through this before. Yes, I love Alexis and I probably always will. She was my first *love*, my *first*, my first *wife*, the mother of my *first* and *only* child. Yes, she has a special place in my heart. I can't help what I feel."

"Does she have first place in your heart now?"

"I'm not going to answer that question, Chaka. We've come too far to revisit all these issues."

A hole ripped through my chest. He had answered my question by not answering it. I wanted to bust out crying, but how could I? I must have known what I was signing up for when I married him.

"I see."

He drove us home.

I faked a headache and cramps in order to avoid intimacy. Calvin brought me two Tylenol and a glass of water. He went back to the living room to watch a football game with his friends.

Finally, I could finish reading the journals to understand how I had come to the point where I would write about what a wonderful husband Calvin was only a few months previously. Maybe the counseling had given us closure on the past. Maybe we really were happy, though I didn't know how I could ever be happy knowing my husband was in love with another woman.

An entry I read shortly before I married Calvin made my plight crystal clear.

Dear Me,

I went to another one of those multi-level-marketing company "business opportunity" meetings today. Daddy's always trying to get in on the bottom floor of the next big pyramid scheme. I didn't sign up to be a representative, but I did learn something they all do: fake it 'til you make it. If you play the part, look the part, and believe the part long enough, eventually your mind will change and you'll make it.

I have decided to fake it until Calvin and I make it. One day, we will wake up and this whole nightmare between him, Alexis, Sierra, even Sandra, and me will be a distant memory.

I have been in love with Calvin since I was sixteen years old. Now is MY time with him, forever.

-Chaka

And from that moment forward, all the writings about Calvin and I were yeah and amen despite the fact that he still cared for Alexis and Sierra like they were his real family. We'd never even put up a Christmas tree in our house was because he'd put up a tree in *Alexis's* apartment. The gifts for Sierra and the rest of his family were under *Alexis's* tree because, one year, Sandra said she wouldn't open up any gift touched by my hands.

Couldn't blame her. Our marriage was all wrong from the get-go, and lying to myself all those years had only made it worse. We were living a fantasy, acting like everything was okay when, in reality, we were both miserable deep down inside.

No wonder I keep my head buried in novels. I'm living in la-la land.

I wasn't sure if our marriage could be saved or if there was anything worth saving. Maybe I should have just released him to go back to his first wife and the family he cherished more than our marriage. Or maybe God could come in and change things around like the pastor had said in the message. I was clueless.

The only thing I did know: I needed some time to reconnect with the real Chaka. The Chaka whose parents taught her right from wrong. The Chaka who revered the institution of marriage. The Chaka who hadn't wrapped herself up in a man who relegated her to second place. Maybe third or fourth—who knows?

Given the fact that Calvin was obviously in Beaver-Cleaver mode, too, I knew he wouldn't understand if I asked for a separation. He would flash that charming smile, say the right words and make me forget we ever had a worry. I was also afraid that he might become extremely angry or even violent, like Dante.

I wondered if I would ever view men the same after being hit by Dante. Baggage.

Speaking of which, I got busy packing. I had to leave Calvin. Maybe not forever, but definitely for today. I stuffed in as many undergarments and warm clothing items as possible.

The layout of the house put our bedroom window at the garage. I could drive to my mother's house and hang out there for a while.

Knowing Calvin, he'd come looking for me and/or put out an APB right away if I didn't somehow let him know that I didn't want to be found. I tore the next empty page from my diary and wrote him a note with a pen I found in our nightstand.

Dear Calvin,

Please don't worry. I'm fine, at least physically. I'm going to get away from "us" for a while. Why, you ask? Because I know you're still madly in love with Alexis. She loves you, too. A part of me almost wants to see you two back together. I'm sorry for what we did to tear your family apart. I know all of that is in the past, but it's not true what they say about the past. It doesn't heal all wounds. It can only heal the wounds we are willing to scrub clean and sanitize, no matter how much it hurts. Otherwise, a nasty wound left to itself becomes infected with the passage of time.

You deserve better. So do I.
-Chaka

I made sure I had a set of keys to some kind of vehicle before I climbed out the window. The actual act of sneaking out wasn't something I had ever experienced before, so I made the mistake of trying to pass my body and my luggage through the window at the same time.

Any fool would have known to throw the suitcase out first. Not me, I had to be hasty.

In one big swoop, I heaved myself over the ledge, but my body weight combined with the bag tilted me over too quickly.

"Wooh!"

Splat! I landed hard on the concrete.

The pain between my eyes told me immediately that I done serious damage to myself.

The concrete faded black.

Chapter 11

Bleep. Bleep. Bleep.

People talking. Don't know who they are.

"The surgery went well."

"Thank God."

"We were able to pinpoint the tear and stop the bleeding."

"Doctor. It's just me and you. Level with me. In your professional opinion, is she going to make it?"

Who is she? What's wrong with her? I hope she makes it.

"It's hard to tell. But she's young. She's strong. In fairly good shape. She's got a good chance of pulling through. You just have to give the brain time to heal itself. Once the swelling goes down, we'll be able to get a better picture of where we stand."

"Best case scenario, will she be the same as she was before the accident, physically and mentally?"

Laughter. "I leave the best case scenarios in God's hands. He's pretty good at those. If there's anyone who can heal Chaka completely, He can."

Chaka! That's me!

Chapter 12

My body jolted forward, sending my mind into panic mode. *What?!*

Brrrt! Brrrrrrrt!

The floor beneath my feet rumbled. Against my will, I jerked forward again. The only thing holding me in place was some kind of strap across my waist.

Seats. Sunlight streaming through rectangular windows. People. *I'm on a plane.*

A second glance around at the spacious seating arrangement revealed something even more interesting: I was seated in *first class* on a plane.

The flight attendant's pleasant voice settled my nerves. "Ladies and gentlemen, on behalf of your Dallas based American Airlines crew, we'd like to welcome you to Dallas/Fort Worth International Airport. ..."

I'm coming home. From where?

The cabin lights suddenly appeared, shining much-needed light on my situation. The young Asian man next to me had to be in his twenties. *A stranger.*

I didn't want to cause commotion on a plane. *Think. Think. My purse!*

For the first time since waking, I took a good look down and realized I could barely *see* down! My body was humongous! I couldn't see my stomach on account of my breasts. I couldn't bend over and feel for my purse on account of my stomach!

"I'll get it for you, Chaka," the Asian man said.

I slammed my back against the seat and faced him. "Are we married?"

He laughed as he reached down where I couldn't. "Perhaps we should be for as much time as we spend together." He pumped his eyebrows in jest, handing me my purse.

Whoever he was, he certainly had a sense of humor. I responded with a silly smirk.

As we taxied to the gate, I imitated the other passengers. My purse, a python-print leather Michael Kors tote, was ridiculously cute. A bag for the bucket list.

I juiced up my phone and saw the notice that I had two voice messages and four texts. My birthday didn't work as a password. Neither did the last four digits of my social security number. At a loss, I put the phone back in my purse. *Here we go again.*

Snippets of the life I had with Byron, Dante and Calvin replayed in my head. I raised my left hand to assess the lifestyle I might be leading, seeing as this designer bag had probably put me back five hundred dollars. Almost the same amount Byron spent on those stupid rims.

No ring. *I'm single.*

Still couldn't believe Byron married Tya Longfield.

My flight companion proved to be quite the gentleman. He slid my bags out of the overhead compartment and stood them in the aisle for me. "Here you go."

I seized the handles, turned sideways and right stepped up middle of the plane toward the runway looking as if I was doing an extended version of the Cupid Shuffle. I promise you, the friction my thighs created could have started a campfire.

I dreaded looking into a mirror, but nature called. My travel partner waited outside the ladies' room with our luggage.

My reflection had to be lying. *No way! What do I do all day—sit around eating Twinkies?* I would not have won any skinny contests in the past, but come on!

A woman one Twinkie ahead of me emerged from a stall. She wore a loose-fitting sweater and a pair of blue jeans, probably stretch-waist.

A double-take of the mirror offered a smidgen of hope. I hadn't let myself go completely. My navy blue suit with silver sequin tank boasted of class and effort.

My Twinkie-twin served herself a helping of soap from the wall-dispenser. She washed her hands in the sink. "They sure don't make these restrooms with women like us in mind," she lamented.

"Mmmm."

I dashed into the stall before I literally wet myself. I squatted over the toilet seat, but my angle must have been off because I felt a warm stream of urine flowing down my thunder thighs.

This bad geometry made me dip down lower. Lower! My muscles screamed from the strain. I posted both elbows on the sides of the stall. They saved my behind from hitting the rim of the public toilet seat, thank God.

This is traumatic. If I had to post signs on street light poles, I was going to find Jabari and hire him to help me shed the extra fifty pounds or so.

I cleaned myself as best as I could and I washed my hands without taking another look at myself.

We had no need to wait for bags, according to my escort/partner/something-other than-my-husband, because we were smart enough to travel light for this trip.

"LaGuardia is no place to wait for luggage if you don't absolutely have to," he said. "I don't have to tell you. You know. I'm glad we were able to leave a day early. Departing on Christmas Eve would have been horrendous."

"So true," I guessed.

An old Tupac song, *Only God Can Judge Me*, began playing from a speaker close by.

"Aren't you going to answer it?" the man asked me. He pointed at my purse.

"Oh. Yes." *Why is Tupac my ringtone?* I rummaged through my phone for a second, scraping toward the sound of the slain rapper's voice. When I found the device, I showed it to my cohort.

He looked at the screen. "Yes! Yes! Yes! She's calling on the business number. Please let me answer it. I've got to get some experience as your assistant," he begged.

I gladly gave him the phone and watched carefully as he traced a circle and the tapped a dot in the center of the circle, unlocking my phone. "Chaka Jones Literary Agency. This is Fang, how may I help you? Yes. Yes. Hold, please."

Fang pressed 'mute'. "It's Stephanie Cole from Miner & Haus Publishing! They're ready to ink the deal with Sister Lover!" He stamped his feet, excited beyond belief.

His enthusiasm nearly caused me to blow my cover. Something inside of me knew that I needed to stay cool, though. "That's wonderful, but I'm just getting off a flight and—."

"Right," Fang snapped into action. "Hi Stephanie. I am certain that Chaka will be elated when she hears the news. Unfortunately, she is still in flight right now. Can I have her call you when she gets settled in?" he paused. "Yes. Give me one second to write the number…"

Fang motioned for me to write. I grabbed a small note pad and pen from my bag.

"212-555-2874."

I recorded as he spoke.

"Thank you so much…Merry Christmas to you, too."

He hung up and quickly asked me, "How was that?"

"Perfect."

He cracked up laughing. "I'm awesome! You're awesome! Oh my gosh, I can't believe I just told the most powerful editor at the biggest publishing house in New York City we'd call her back at *our* convenience. This amazing! Unheard of in our industry!" He raised his hand for a high-five.

I slapped his palm, wondering what on earth would possess me to pass up an opportunity to speak to this Stephanie woman? During my two years of college—the ones I remembered from the life I had with Byron—I wrote a novel. I'd submitted it to three publishers. All three turned it down. I got a nibble from a fourth publisher at a smaller house who gave me several tips for polishing the book. "I'd like to take a look at the manuscript again after you make the changes."

"You can do this, babe!" Byron had cheered me on. "You're a great writer!" Of course, he would say so after all the papers I practically wrote for him.

I had every intention of rewriting the book and sending it in again. But just a few weeks later, I discovered I was pregnant. My entire focus shifted from pursuing my hopes and dreams to managing the practicalities of life.

And today, here I was passing up a call from Miner & Haus? *Am I crazy?*

Listening to Fang all the way home answered my question. I wasn't crazy – I *was* awesome, just like he had said. Turns out, Fang was a university intern who was working at *my* esteemed agency to make connections in the publishing industry and learn the ropes from none other than Miss Chaka Jones, celebrity literary agent.

Wow! I'm at the top of my career!

He went on and on about how wonderful it was to work with me and how honored he was to drive me from DFW back to our office. I glanced at the digital clock near the radio dial. *3:07pm. Why are we going back to the office this late in the afternoon, especially since tomorrow is Christmas Eve?*

The thought occurred to me that maybe we had a ridiculously demanding boss. Then I remembered: I *am* the boss.

Fang maneuvered the metroplex highways until we hit I-75. We exited Arapaho Road. A few quick turns and we were at the office. *My business.* Chaka Jones Literary Agency.

The moment Fang and I walked through the door, the modest suite came alive with activity.

"Hello, Chaka! Welcome back!" from the receptionist, a woman dressed in all black, yet wearing bright red lipstick in contrast. She was fashionable and sophisticated, the kind of young lady one would expect to encounter in the literary industry. An artist who took care of business.

I smiled at her. "Hello."

Her eyes widened, as though surprised I had spoken to her.

Next, a man wearing tight skinny jeans, an argyle vest and a turtleneck approached me with a manila file. "We've got an offer for the tell-all book from Miley Cyrus's best friend."

"Her best friend?" I wondered openly.

Fang announced, "People! We just walked in the door. Let the woman breathe first! He grabbed my elbow and escorted me down the hallway with the rest of my luggage.

He's so dramatic.

"I'll be right back," I called to my employees even as Fang whisked me away to my headquarters. He whispered to me, "Listen, Chaka, I know we've been out of town for a couple of days and there's a lot to catch up on, but you and I both know that your first priority is returning Stephanie's call asap."

He dropped off his notebook at his desk, then basically shoved me into my office. "I won't let anyone in until you're finished," he guaranteed from the other side of the door.

My office. The executive furniture was classy, but my desk was a mess. Piles of papers on top of a calendar I could barely see. An empty Starbucks container. Pens and highlighters strewn across the 8-foot surface.

Behind my desk, however, was a glass shelving unit with various trophies on display. I dropped my purse in the main chair and examined the awards.

Best Literary Agency – Southwest, Top Producing Literary Agent, Texas Business Women's Hall of Fame, Trailblazer Award, The Go-Getter Trophy, Distinguished Alumni Award.

This was only the top row. My chubby face graced the covers of state and national magazines honoring businesswomen and literary executives.

There were also photos of me with various celebrities—music, sports, acting, reality TV—holding books. I assumed all those deals had been inked with my help.

The magazine covers and photos had been professionally framed and posted conspicuously around my office. My college degrees were also obnoxiously present on my walls.

Dang! I'm at the top of my game! This is the life!

Tupac's lyrics brought a halt to my train of thought. I examined the screen. *Stephanie - Miner & Haus. What do I say?* My life was going so well, I didn't want to mess it up. Neither did I want to lose this deal, according to Fang. I had to answer. "Hello?"

"Chaka, Darling, hope you had a wonderful flight back to Dallas," she opened the conversation.

"Yes. It was great, thank you."

"Are you ready to talk business?"

"Certainly," I hoped.

"Are you looking at the contract now?"

Duh! "Just a second."

I mashed the "mute" button and ran out of my office, which put me at Fang's desk. "I've got Stephanie on the line. I need to see the contract."

Fang opened his desk drawer and whipped out a 20-page legal document. "Something told me to make another copy."

"Thank you so much, Fang. You're a lifesaver."

He beamed with pride. "I try."

Okay, now he's just kissing up.

I returned to my desk and resumed the call. "I've got it."

"Okay," Stephanie said, "we can make the changes to clause seven, no problem."

I checked the corresponding number on the contract, skimming through the noted changes with my initials next to them. "Got it."

"Numbers fifteen and nineteen, we're okay with the counter of a four hundred thousand dollar advance, but we'd like to bump the tiered bonuses up per two hundred thousand copies, and bring the bonus down to twenty thousand."

"Ummmm…" I stalled as I quickly read the statement she was talking about. From what I gathered, in the original contract Sister Lover would get a $300,000 advance and another $25,000 bonus after 150,000 books were sold. Now, they were agreeing to my request to pay $400,000 up front. But they weren't going to keep to the original bonus structure. This was all a matter of how much money my client would get in the end.

If I was as good as all those awards said I was, I needed to come back with something more in my client's favor. "How about giving the bonus at 175,000 copies sold instead of 200,000?"

Stephanie sighed. "You're really pushing it, Chaka."

"I know. That's what I do best."

"Ugh," she breathed. "Okay. Number thirty-one."

Stephanie and I talked for another thirty minutes, hammering out the details of Sister Lover's book deal. Basically, whatever Stephanie wanted, I gave her a little less, and vice versa. We met somewhere in the middle. No different than compromising with a husband, from what I recalled.

She said she'd do her best to push the revised contract through the first week in January so we could secure the deal by the middle of next month.

"Great," I agreed, guessing this was standard. "Have a great Christmas break."

"You, too," Stephanie said. "And listen, I hear you've got something about Miley Cyrus?"

"We've already got an offer on that one," I said. But then, I remembered how fabulous I was. "But if Miner and Hause can beat it, I'm certainly willing to listen."

Stephanie gave a patronizing laugh. "They don't call you Chaka the shark for nothing. Let's talk next week. Merry Christmas, Chaka."

"Merry Christmas to you, too, Stephanie."

Chaka the shark?

Fang must have been listening to our conversation, because the moment I got off the phone with Stephanie, he came busting through the door. "How did it go?"

"It's finished."

"Yes! Yes! Yes!" he danced his little jig again. "I knew it!"

I'm sure you did.

"Okay, okay," he said calmly, cupping my hands with his. "Okay, Miss Chaka. In light of this beautiful, wonderful deal...I have a special request."

I squinted, tilting my head to the side. "Yyyyyes?"

"On behalf of myself and everyone else in this office..." He rubbed the back of my hands gently.

"Out with it, already, Fang."

"Is-there-*any*-possible-way-we-could-have-off-tomorrow-for-Christmas-Eve?" he blurted out.

My face squashed in, involuntarily. *Why wouldn't my staff be off for Christmas Eve?*

"Wait! Before you say no, hear me out," Fang pleaded. "I'll take the Mary J. Blige manuscript home with me to read. Jacquelyn will complete the edits for the Romo book...we've got it covered. We'll get the work done over the holiday. It's just that," he continued with desperately, "the weather might get bad, and—"

"Fang. It's okay," I stopped him before he could throw in something about Santa, "You guys can take off Christmas Eve. And don't take all this work with you. You should be enjoying your friends and families over the break. Take off now, if you'd like."

Fang kissed me on both cheeks. "I'm so sorry, but thank you! Thank you! Thank you!"

I walked back into my office and fell into my seat. *I really am Chaka the shark.* I listened as my employees rejoiced over the good news. I overheard one of them make a half-serious joke, "We'd better get out of here before she changes her mind." After wishing each other and me a Merry Christmas, they cleared out of there in no time flat.

Too bad I hadn't bothered to get my home address from Fang before I let him go. It took me nearly two hours to get an address for myself, which I finally uncovered from an old email confirming my apartment rent had been paid.

If I'm so awesome, why do I live in an apartment?

Through my phone's map app, I routed from my office location to my residence and found my answer. I lived at *The Rowlett* Luxury Apartment Community, near Victory Park. My complex was one of those swanky downtown high-rises—the ones where they charge *more* to leave the walls half-finished.

My phone vibrated with a text from Fang. *I took the Romo manuscript anyway because it needs to be finished by Monday. I left the Katy Mary for you. Merry Christmas! XOXOX!*

As much as I wanted to get a look at my apartment, I'll be the first to admit: I was a *for-reeeal* Katy Mary fan.

She was *the* top Christian vocalist and her songs always made me feel like Jesus Himself was sitting next to me.

I searched through the stacks and found the one with her name on the cover. With pleasure, I dove headfirst into what I thought would be an autobiographical account of her life. However, the notes in the margins soon gave away the whole charade. A ghostwriter had written Katy Mary's book, someone named Jackson. Jackson had a ton of questions that Katy needed to answer. It was my job at this point to read the manuscript as-is and make executive decisions about cuts before bothering Katy's people with the questions that required her response.

"Awww, man. This whole thing is fake," I said to myself.

I felt around my desk for something more authentic to read. Something juicy, perhaps, worthy of a reality show. Underneath two other piles, I found my diary. Again.

The Diary of Chaka Jones. A quick flip through revealed very few entries.

March 14

Dear Me,

Sorry I haven't written much. Too busy. Talk to you later.

-Chaka

November 28

Dear Me,

In New York. Missed Thanksgiving with the family. Mom is not talking to me. I have to make it up to her some kind of way whenever I get the chance. Don't know why she can't just be happy for my success!

-Chaka

December 20
Dear Me,

Got a new intern. He's wired, but I like his enthusiasm. Business is great. Mike and I are back together again. Don't ask me why. Lost 3 pounds last week. Gained 4 this week.

-Chaka

I heard the door to my office suite open. "Hello?"

"Hello!" someone called back to me.

A man wearing a dark blue jumpsuit with "Omar" embroidered on a white oval, obviously a work uniform entered my office. "Evening. I knew you'd still be here. All work and no play. I'll start cleaning in the front rooms."

All work and no play? In light of his words, I took a second look around my office. There were no beach vacation photos. No cruise ship shots. Most of all, no pictures with friends and family.

I shuffled the Katy Mary manuscript back into a single stack and stuffed it into a large white envelope. I searched my desk for other urgent-looking documents, then corralled them all into the luggage I still had sitting near the door.

"I think I'll head on home, now," I yelled over Omar's vacuum. "Merry Christmas."

"What? You leaving already?"

"Already."

Chapter 13

There were only three cars left in the business park parking lot. I pushed the "unlock" button on my Lexus key fob and, thankfully, a pair of lights flickered, guiding me to my vehicle. I owned a white two-dour coupe with tan interior. *Nice.*

As I approached the Victory Park area of Dallas, traffic slowed to a snail's pace. *What's going on here?* Thirty minutes later, I understood by shoe polish scribblings on car windows, that I was in the middle of concert traffic for a band by the name of "Whooty-Whoo." All I could do was take note of the fandom because if I didn't get a literary contract after all the time I spent in the wake of their concert, this would be the biggest waste of time ever.

Finally, I reached The Rowlett, which was every bit as grand as its pictures online. The only problem was: I had no idea where to park. I ambled over to the main entrance. Before I could power my window down, some man wearing all black rushed up to me and tried to open my driver's door.

Is he trying to car-jack me right in front of my complex?

I was preparing to scream when he said, "Good evening, Miss Chaka."

"Oh. Hi."

"I'll take it from here."

It's valet.

"Right."

Another man wearing a three-piece suit and a hat approached me and offered to take my bags. I'm sorry, but I had to turn him down because no matter how much money I made, I wasn't going to spend all my cash tipping folks.

Maybe this isn't my home. Perhaps it was a hotel, because I'd only seen bellhops and valets the few times Byron and I had traveled and stayed in nice places.

I tipped the driver and carried on to my new and improved lifestyle. The building's interior should have been on a postcard. Sleek blue loungers, tall columns, a giant fish tank that took up almost an entire wall. Enough space and elegance to throw a presidential ball.

"Miss Jones!" a woman behind the "Concierge" stand called me.

"Yes?"

"Welcome home. I believe Lonnie held a package for you." She indicated the door to my right.

"Thank you."

I drug the bags with me into what was obviously the office area. Upon entrance, a man with spiked hair and way-too-tanned skin greeted me. "Hi Chaka!"

Thank God for nametags. "Hi, Lonnie. How are you?"

"Wonderful! Did you close another deal in New York?"

"As a matter of fact, I did!"

He stepped back and looked me up and down. "Cool! Can you share details yet?"

"Um…no. I can't possibly leak the news." I batted my eyes.

"Bummer," he whined. "I'll have to wait until it hits the bookstores. Your clients' books are always so juicy and scandalous. I love 'em."

"Oh. Well…great. Thank you." *Whatever happened to literature?*

"What's with the humility today?"

"I'm just tired." *At my size, who wouldn't be?*

"I see. I'd be dirt-tired if I lived your busy life." There was a twinge of brown-nosing in his tone. I wondered if everyone in my circle was a "yes person".

"You've got a package for me?" I moved the conversation along.

"Yes! Almost forgot." He ducked into his office, then returned with an oversized manila envelope. "Feels like another manuscript from another famous client."

The only information that interested me on the package was my apartment number. 2102. *The twenty-first floor!* "Thanks, Lonnie. Have a good day."

I propped the envelope under my armpit, grabbed the luggage handgrips, and headed toward an area where I thought an elevator might be. Instead, I found the gym. This was a good thing. I made a mental note of its location, hoping a membership was included in whatever outrageous monthly fee I must have been paying to live in such a beautiful, well-staffed residence.

Past the gym came the elevators. One for the first twelve floors, another for top floors. I pressed the arrow button and waited along with two high-fashion, model-types who jabbered away about a party tonight on the outdoor terrace. Groupies.

The elevator arrived with a ding. Two men in casual khakis and one lady with her puffy white Bichon Frise stepped off. The other two ladies and I boarded.

The door was almost closed when a man's voice called, "Hold the elevator!"

One of the women pressed the button that sent the doors sliding open.

I recognized the voice before I saw the face. My arms pimpled. In stepped Dante.

I pressed my back against the wall opposite the control panel and slid my sunglasses onto my face.

"Hello," he spoke to them. He made brief eye contact with me. Nodded. Not a spark of recognition.

My breath returned.

"Oh my gosh!" one of the women nearly screamed. "Aren't you Dante Lewis?"

He smiled. "Yes."

"You are so amazing to watch," her friend said, her eyes glazed over. "You're, like, my dad's idol. He would lay down his life for you."

Your Daddy is a nut.

"Thank you. But it's…you know…a sport. At the end of the day, I'm a regular guy, you know?" he said wearing that same fake, deceiving grin.

"Your family must sooo appreciate what you do," from the first one again.

I couldn't hold it any longer. "Do you beat your wife?"

"What?"

The fans inhaled sharply. "Oh my gosh."

I stepped toward him. "I said, do you beat your wife? Do you hit her? And your little boy?"

"Ma'am, I'm not married," he stated. "No kids, either."

I blinked three times and resumed my spot against the wall. "Oh. Sorry."

The twenty-first floor took forever to come. I was thankful that the other women hadn't exited and left me there alone with him.

Too embarrassed to say goodbye, I just rolled myself and my luggage right on off the elevator when I got to my floor. Seven doorways down on the left, I stuck several different keys into the hole before it finally opened.

And there was my magnificent, albeit tiny, apartment. Standing in one spot, I took in the granite slab countertops, stainless steel appliances, and European-style cabinetry in the kitchen. I could also see the garden tub in my bathroom.

Simply gorgeous, and obviously professionally decorated. *Can't wait to see the bedroom.*

But when I opened the door I suspected contained my bed, I got an eye full of some man's naked backside, and he was obviously *very* occupied with a woman in bed.

Roommates!

I slammed the door shut. "I'm sorry!" I yelled to them. "Chaka!"

He don't need to be yellin' my name right now.

I heard a thud. Glass crashed on the hardwood floor.

Concerned, I approached the door cautiously. "Are you guys okay?"

The door swung open and the man's companion fled the apartment while he and I stood facing one another at the door to the bedroom door. "Chaka, this is *not* what it looks like."

"Who *are* you?" I started the awkward conversation.

"I know, right?" Every freckle on his high yellow face slid a quarter inch. With one hand clutching the covers, he only had one hand free to animate his words. "This is completely out of character for me, but believe me when I tell you, she means nothing to me. *Nothing*!"

"What do *I* mean to you?"

"Chaka, you are everything to me!" He drew a big, round circle in the air. "You are the sun, the stars, and the moon in my life, sweetheart. You *have* to believe me."

I'd been in his presence for less than five minutes and I already knew he was lying through his pearly whites. "You must be my no-good, cheating boyfriend. I haven't had one of those in a long time," I laughed.

He stepped toward me. The covers fell to the floor as he pressed his body against mine. He put both hands on my cheeks. I squirmed out of his reach, thinking about germ transference. "Ewww! Gross! You just got out of bed with somebody! Don't touch me!"

I rushed to the bathroom and scrubbed my face clean with the fancy bottle of facial cleanser on the counter. The plush towel on the ring smelled of flowery fabric softener. *Who does my laundry?*

Old boy barged into the restroom wearing a pair of boxers. "Chaka, talk to me. Please. We can work through this."

I had only one more question for him. "Whose apartment is this?"

His face filled with fear. "Baby, I know you pay all the bills, but—"

"What? I pay *all* the bills? You don't pay *nothin'*?"

He tried again, "I pay my *love*."

I cracked up laughing in his face. I mean, a big old belly-aching laugh, and right about then, I had plenty of belly. "Woo, oh my gosh. What's your name?"

"Mike."

"Oh, Mike." I put my hand on his shoulder. "*That* was hilarious. Now get out."

He called me everything but a child of God, plus every fat-phrase he could think of. Told me I was lucky to have a man, as big as I was.

I didn't care, so long as he kept stuffing clothes in those trash bags. Then he had the nerve to ask for one more chance.

"Mmmmm." I rolled my eyes to the left, pretending to reconsider. "Nope."

The way he pranced out my apartment, I had to wonder if he was somehow related to Fang.

I didn't know what kind of relationship-foolishness I had allowed before, but fat or not, I was not going to allow myself to be used and abused anymore. Not me. Not Chaka "The Shark" Jones.

My stomach growled and, suddenly, I realized I had been so busy, I hadn't eaten anything all afternoon. The hunger led me straight to the pantry which was, surprisingly, quite bare. A package of almonds, some honey buns, some mix-and-match canned foods and noodles that were probably extras from meals long past. My refrigerator wasn't much better. Water. Lemonade. Bananas that needed to be thrown out.

I carefully picked up the stem of the bananas and pressed the lever to throw them into my trashcan. That's when I noticed the Styrofoam containers and fast food sandwich wrappers. *Now I get why I'm so big – I'm always eating out.* I had never been one to count calories or carbs, but I would definitely do myself a favor and get some groceries in my cushy joint so I wouldn't have to leave my health to the fast food fairy.

For tonight, however, pizza delivery would have to do.

The bags I'd brought home were still at the bedroom door. I rolled them into my bedroom. After changing my linens and taking a shower, I unpacked. My jaw fell open when I saw "Size 20" on my pants label. Momma wore a size 20. *She must have something smart to say every time she sees me now.*

When the pizza arrived, I ate one slice and threw the rest away because there was no way I could carry on in size 20. But then something amazing happened. My body would not allow me to stop eating. I mean, the hunger was unreal. Unnatural. Like I had been programmed to overeat, somehow. I had heard about people's systems getting reconfigured by all the fancy engineering that goes into well-advertised foods, but I knew it for myself now. *I need to write a book about* this!

Three slices later, I found myself back in my room lying on my bed watching television feeling like a straight up slug. It was all I could do to drag the manuscript out of my attaché and sit it on my bed.

The package I had received at the front desk was also in my reach, so I hoisted it onto the bed as well, with great difficulty.

Beeeelllch!

I opened the delivered package to see exactly how much more work I had lined up for me.

When I finally took a moment to read the sender's name, I nearly lost the food in my stomach.

The package was from Daddy.

Chapter 14

My hands trembled as I tore through the brown paper, afraid of what I might find. The box had been secured with layers of tape, which required the use of my keys to break through. Finally, I brushed past the tissue paper, exposing a leopard-print scarf with a matching hat and gloves. A classic three-piece gift set from any major department store.

This was Momma's style of gift-giving. *Is this some kind of bad joke?* Under the last garment, I found a hand-written note from Daddy.

Chaka,

Your Momma's too upset with you to send this gift right now, so I sent it on behalf of all of us. Since you didn't come home for Thanksgiving and don't know if you will be back be Christmas, we are going up to Denver to visit your sister. We love you. See you when we get back.

-Daddy

I couldn't find my cell phone fast enough. I had to draw the symbol three times before my phone accepted the code. 214-555-9120.

"Hello?" Momma's voice answered.

"Hi, Momma."

"Well, look what the cat done drug through the phone," she chided.

"Momma, I'm sorry. I should have been there for Thanksgiving," I apologized readily.

"Hmph. I wasn't expecting those words from you," she said, probably disappointed that she didn't have the chance to fuss at me more. My Momma was…well, my Momma.

Still unsure of what to think about the note in Daddy's script, I fished, "Umm…Momma…about Daddy…"

"What about him?"

"Is he…was he…"

"Here. You talk to him."

I froze.

"Y'llo," rang the familiar voice.

I wailed, "Daddy, Daddy, Daddy. It's *you*, Daddy," as a river of tears flowed from my eyes.

"Wait a minute here, baby girl, you alright?"

The heaving wouldn't subside. "I"—huh, huh—"love"—huh, huh—"you, Daddy." I broke all the way down to the ugly-cry. Daddy tried to shush me, but there was no end in sight.

"I love you, too, Chaka, now come on, here. Pull yourself together and tell me what's wrong?" he coaxed, fear tracing his words.

Momma hopped on the phone. "Chaka, what's the problem? You havin' a nervous breakdown?"

"No! Put Daddy back on the phone!" I screamed at her.

"You keep this up, I'm gonna call that con-surge man at your apartment and see if he need to call 9-1-1 on you."

"O-o-okay," I managed to say as I tried to get a grip on myself. "I'm okay, Momma, put Daddy back on the phone. Please."

"Baby girl, you calmed down now?" he asked.

"Daddy, I'm coming to Denver on the next flight out of Dallas."

"Not possible. Airport's shut down 'cause of the weather. Me and your Momma got in just in time," he informed me.

"No!" I squealed. "God, why?"

"God's in control of the weather, Chaka. He's got this," Daddy reassured me in his deep, loving tone. "You still haven't told me what the problem is."

"Daddy, I miss you," I babbled.

"I miss you, too. We *all* miss you. Don't get me wrong, we're all proud of your success and all, but I'd be lying if I said I don't get jealous of that company of yours," he chuckled.

"I'll close it! I don't care!"

"Whoa now, hold your horses. Don't get carried away. You just need to balance, honey. You done put everything on hold tryin' to conquer the world," he explained. "Went straight from high school to college, finished college early, went right to graduate school, straight to New York to launch your company. You ain't hardly had time for a life outside of work."

My wits returned enough to carry me to the kitchen for a glass of water. I sat on a bar stool, listening to my father's counsel even as my heart broke. If my literary agent life ended, like the one with Byron, Dante, and Calvin, this might be the last conversation I would have with my father.

"So what should I do? I mean, I *love* owning my own company, having my own money, living this wonderful life. But…Daddy, I know now that time is precious." I held off another wave of hysterics. "And once you're gone, I can't get you back again."

He coughed.

I gasped. "Daddy! Are you sick?"

He cleared his throat. "Got this tickle in my chest. Coughing every now and then. Little fever. Your Momma's been giving me green tea with lemon and—"

"You need to go to the doctor," I barked in a manner that was awfully close to being disrespectful but I didn't care. My father had ignored the signs of pneumonia until it was too late.

And he replied the same way he had in my life with Byron. "Doctors don't know what they're doing half the time. All of 'em crooks, if you ask me. Especially once you get on Medicare. Tryin' to keep us here longer than the Lord wants us here, I think."

"But Daddy, don't you *want* to stay alive?" I pleaded for his life.

"No longer than I'm supposed to. I know where I'm going when this is all over. Long as I get to see to my girls are taken care of, I can rest in peace."

I bargained with him, "Are you saying that if I never get married, you'll fight to live?"

"Naw, you don't have to be married for me to know you're taken care of. To me, when I can see you've got your relationship with Christ underway, when I know you put yourself in *His* care, then I'll know you're alright," Daddy said. I could hear him smile.

"Daddy, that's a trick. If I give myself to God, then I'll lose you," I said.

"That ain't no trick. You give yourself to Him, and we'll always share His Spirit – love. Now and forever."

I still couldn't believe I was actually talking to my father on the phone. I wanted to holler, cry again, reach through the phone and pull close to his neck one more time so I could smell his Old Spice aftershave.

"And another thing," he continued, "since you brought it up, you ain't gettin' no younger. High tide you started lookin' to settle down."

"Daddy, you would be so appalled to know what I've been dealing with lately," I stated.

"No, not really, honey. I know you've kissed a lot of frogs between Dallas and New York," he teased. Coughed again.

I had to try. "*Please* go see a doctor."

"Don't try to change the subject," he ignored me. "Now. I'm glad you didn't marry that Mike fellow and I hope to God you don't take up with him again."

"Mike and I are through, Daddy," I assured him. "Do you remember Calvin?"

"Oh, yeah, baby, I'm sorry you had to go through all that," he said in a low tone. "I'm just glad you got out of there without a baby.

"Mmmm."

"You know who I really liked for you?" he asked.

"That one boy you met in college. I think…his name is…Byron! That was it."

Tears of squeaked through my eyes, "Daddy, you liked Byron?"

"Oh yeah," he said authoritatively. "He was good people. And I know you wasn't crazy about him because he wasn't flashy or slick, wasn't no ladies' man you had to fight over. Ask me, you probably been watchin' too many TV shows to recognize a good 'un. But don't worry, God will send you another one."

Cough. Cough. Cough-cough-cough.

I held my breath. *God, why?*

"Daddy? Daddy!"

He recovered. "I'm right here, Chaka. But it's getting late."

"No, please…no."

"We can talk tomorrow," he said.

"But tomorrow isn't promised."

"You're right about that," he agreed. "All we've got is today. And we need to make the best of whatever God allows *today* 'cause whatever He allows, He will use to shape you into the person He wants you to be. Right now, He's shaping me toward the bed. I'm startin' to get the chills. I gotta go."

My heavy-breathing cry cranked up. "Daddy, wait."

He coughed, almost angrily this time. "What is it?"

Nothing seemed more important than to tell him that I loved him again.

"I love you, too, baby girl. Good night."

Maybe it was a good thing he hung up before my wailing started again. If these were his last days, I didn't want him worrying about my well-being.

After a second meltdown, curled up in my bed, I scrounged up the wherewithal to get on my phone and double-check flights to Denver. Daddy was right. I couldn't even find a private charter to get me to anywhere near Colorado.

My Daddy is alive and I can't see him. I was on the heels of meltdown number three. I slid onto the floor, landing on my knees, with my elbows on the bed. "God, why? Why would you let this happen to me?"

Wait a minute—didn't I say these same words in all the other lives? No life I live is ever good enough for me.

My tears came to an abrupt halt as I replayed what happened with Byron. We were a normal couple, a normal family facing financial challenges. Dante, as throwed-off as he was, needed help. Despite the fact that our marriage was ridiculous, I'd still have to raise Michaela and DJ with him. And even though Calvin was still in love with Alexis, he and I were in holy covenant together. We needed serious deliverance. My life as a woman married to my career came with its trade-off, too.

In every life, I had been unsatisfied.

So maybe the problem wasn't the life that God allowed. The problem was how I faced it. Without hope. Without Him.

I clasped my hands. "God, I don't know what's going on here or if all of this is even real. All I know is that I need you. Whatever I face, whatever I'm going through. All my disappointments. All my dreams. All my hopes. God, I give them to you. Whatever You allow is what I will give thanks in. Even if you take my Daddy again…" I had to stop for a moment and work through that one. "Even when you take him, I will find my hope and my life in Christ, now and forever. In Jesus name, Amen."

I sat on the floor for a while longer, waiting for my mind to settle. Stepping outside on my terrace provided a beautiful view of the Dallas skyline. I breathed in the crisp night air, letting it fill my lungs and rush through my system.

The heaviness in my heart for my father still existed, but the truth bore the bulk of the weight for me. If I never spoke to my father again in this life, he would be waiting, with Jesus, on the other side.

In the meanwhile, I wanted to enjoy my life. Enjoy the talents God had given me, and live not for tomorrow but for today.

A quick Google search produced a phone number for Byron Stringer. I paid the $49 via my a pre-existing credit card linked to my phone and snooped further into the life of the Byron Stringer of Dallas who shared the same birthdate as the one I remembered.

He was single. Never been married. Worked a blue-collar job. No history of arrests. And his phone number was listed. I pressed the number listed on the screen. My dialer asked if I wanted to call.

Yes.

"Hello?" he answered.

"Hi. Byron."

"Huh?"

"Byron…Byron?…Byron!"

Chapter 15

"Byron! Byron!"

"Baby, I'm right here," he whispered into my ear.

I tried to open my eyes, but the bright lights shot through, sending what felt like a knife through my brain.

"Mother, go get the doctor. She's awake," he yelled with excitement, which sent another dagger through my skull.

"Not so loud."

"Momma. You're up?"

I felt my son's cool hands shaking my arm.

"Don't shake her, London."

True to his style, he didn't listen. I turned my head to face him, letting some light beyond my lids. "Yes, London. I'm up," I answered. He wouldn't have stopped otherwise. *That's my London.*

Doctors and nurses flew in like a tornado, documenting my vitals, pinching me here and there, asking me a ton of questions: Do you know what year it is? Who is the President of the United States? Do you know what month it is?

My boys cheered with each correct answer.

I must have fallen asleep again because when I opened my eyes, the room was dark except for a tiny Christmas tree in the corner twinkling with lights. I shifted my neck to get a better look at it.

"Charka," Byron's gentle voice called my name. "You up?"

He was posted up in a chair beside my bed with two blankets covering him. The Byron I remember was always cold. Sleeping in the cool hospital room with me had been a sacrifice.

He stood over me. Though his face was a shadow, I could tell his eyes were puffy. Perhaps from lack of sleep. Maybe weeping, I couldn't be sure.

"Thank you for being here," I muttered.

A smile spread from ear to ear on his face. "Merry Christmas, baby." He kissed me softly on the forehead. Rubbed my head with his hand.

"Merry Christmas to you, Byron. Where are the boys?"

"With your mom."

"Mmmm." I swallowed. Tasted like zombie-spit, I promise. "My throat is dry."

Byron poured me a cup of water and held the straw still so I could take a sip. "Thank you."

"I was hoping you'd wake up again before midnight. I brought your present."

He walked to the tree, bent down to pick up the lone box underneath it, and transported it back to me. He switched on a lamp, one he'd brought from the house.

I tried to lift my hands, but the effort was too much. "Open it for me."

"You sure?"

"Yeah."

He took his sweet time, playing peek-a-boo with the gift.

"Stop. Come on, Byron, quit playing."

He cheezed. "You ready for this?"

"Yes," my vocal chords were in full effect now.

He ripped the wrapping paper down the middle. *Is that what I think it is?*

"Ta-daa!" he proudly finished the reveal.

"A laptop?" I sat up slightly.

"Yep. A laptop. For you."

"Byron, we don't have that kind of money, especially not after those rims—"

"I'll be sure to tell the doctor that your memory is completely in tact, woman," he mocked.

I wanted to be happy about the present, but a brand new laptop still in the box was way too expensive for our budget. "Byron, honey…"

"Wait." He put a finger on my lips. "First things first. I didn't buy rims for my car at Kindall's. This *laptop* is what I bought for *you* at Kindall's. I had to say something to cover up."

"Awww, Byron. That was sweet of you." *But this, too, is going back.*

He must have sensed my dismay. He pulled a stool close and sat next to me, still holding the laptop. "Chaka, listen." My husband's eyes moistened. "I know you gave up a lot when we got pregnant in college. I knew you had dreams. I knew you always wanted to be writer. You wanted to earn a college degree. That didn't happen, and I'm partly responsible.

"I know things have been really hard on you, raising the boys, with London's special challenges. I was kind of upset when you decided to get a second job to provide what I couldn't. I could just see that you weren't happy." He wiped his eyes and should have wiped mine, too.

"Well, anyway, baby, I got this laptop because I want to give you back your dreams. You can use it to write a book, go back to school, or whatever. Be everything God wants you to be. Go for it, babe. I believe in you."

My Lord, I must have boo-hooed for a good five minutes while hugging Byron.

"Baby, I didn't know you were gonna react like this," he laughed uncomfortably.

"Byron, you don't know the half. I want to apologize, too. I've been walking around having this huge pity party, thinking my life would have been better if I'd done this or that. Sulking over the shoulda, woulda, couldas, you know?"

He nodded. "Yeah. I know."

"Whatever has happened is what God allowed. Might not have been His perfect will, but He *did* allow it. My father told me, one time, that God only allows detours that will bring us to His expected end, like He said in Jeremiah 29:11. And I feel like where we are, right here, right now, is exactly where God wanted me to arrive."

"Whew," Byron whistled. "All of this over a laptop?"

"You could say that."

Both my earthly father and my Heavenly Father had been right about Byron.

"Okay," I finally released my husband from the firm grip I'd locked him in. "We can keep it. I love you, Byron."

"I love you, too, Chaka."

I sniffed. "Byron?"

"Yes?"

"You still think Tya Longfield has rabbit teeth, right?"

Epilogue

June 9

Dear Me,

Once I woke up from the sleep, I recovered quite nicely. The medical bills came rolling in with a vengeance. Of course, we didn't have the money to pay them. But in the time I took to recover, I was able to sit at home all day and write, write, write while drawing unemployment. I wrote two novellas and published them online. To my surprise, people actually bought them...a lot of people! Enough to start paying our car note and free up money for the medical bills. We still have a long way to go, but I still have, like, fifty more books in me at least.

The first person to write a review was Felecia, from my old job. I sent her an email to thank her. She was always so enamored by my life – can you believe it?

Even though not a whole lot has actually changed yet on the money-front, I feel hopeful. Just the idea that things can get better is helping.

And hope does not disappoint because of the best gift of all, Jesus Christ.

It's Christmas every day in my heart.

Thank you, Father.

-Chaka

~

A Note from the Author

If you have yet to start your journey in Christ, let me encourage you to seek Him. Seek Him in all of his glory, all of His love, and His wisdom. If you feel the tug in your heart, Thank Him for His goodness, ask Him for forgiveness, and invite Him to live in you. He stands knocking on the door of your heart and is more than pleased to come in and be your Lord (Rev. 3:20).

Want More from Michelle Stimpson?
You'll love the bestselling, award-winning Mama B
Novella series!
Over 100 5-Star Reviews on Amazon!

Here's Chapter 1 of Mama B: A Time to Speak

If Rev. Omar hollers one more time that it's gonna be hotter than this in hell, I'm going to have to walk out of this sanctuary. I, for one, don't plan on spending no time in hell. No sense in gettin' prepared for a place you ain't goin' to.

I kept my feet still, though. He was trying, bless his heart. And it wasn't his fault somebody stole all the copper out the church's air conditioning system the night before. People ought to have more respect for the house of God. But I guess when some folks get broke and their babies start crying for milk, don't matter to them how they get the money so long as they get it.

I'd already asked the Lord to touch the rascal who took the copper; give him a mind to work an honest job and let somebody hire him. Either that or put him in jail so he can't mess up nobody else's air.

Rev. Martin said the thief was probably somebody on drugs who needed quick money. "All these Dallas folks movin' into town," he had fussed earlier while we rummaged through the storage looking for fans and Kleenexes before the service started. "They bring the dope and the crime problems with 'em."

"You sure right about that," Mother Ophelia Pugh seconded. "I wish they'd find some place else to move. Peasner gettin' way too crowded for me."

"Where else you want 'em to go?" I laughed quietly.

"I don't know, Beatrice, just not here."

Peasner had always been a good spot to live. Folk got along with each other, for the most part. We was close enough to the city to have a good doctor and mighty fine shopping; far enough out to not need an alarm system for your house. People still knew each other—families, businesses and whatnot. At least that's the way it used to be. But since they put that highway loop through Peasner, seem like a whole lot of restaurants poppin' up. New houses going up so fast, make your head swim.

Ophelia passed me another unopened tissue box. These would come in handy when folks got to sweating. "Sister, I like that suit. Sharp! Tell you what, B, if I lose about fifty pounds, I'mma have to come make my home in your closet."

I shooed at her. "Please, Ophelia. You know as well as I do, they make pretty clothes for all sizes. Not like back when all you could buy was a muumuu, over size fourteen."

Ophelia pulled the light switch and stepped down off the stool. "That's it. No more Kleenexes."

I looked down at the four boxes in my hand and shook my head. The church had nine pews on each side. On a regular Sunday, all but the last couple of rows would be at least half full. I figured once folks got to standing and clapping and carrying on, we'd need a whole lot more than those few tissues and funeral home fans to keep them from passing out.

Now back in my day, before we had air conditioning, we could worship the Lord all day at church with just the breezes flowing through the open windows.

We were used to high temperatures. I do believe God graced us for the Texas heat before He let us figure out how to beat it.

Don't get me wrong, though, I likes my air conditioner. My late husband, Albert, used to fuss—ooh, Lord, that man could fuss—about me running the air twenty-four hours a day. We never could agree on what degrees the house should be.

I sure do miss fussin' with Albert.

Well, anyway, I already knew those folk sure would be fussin' that Sunday. Had to go on and get my mind ready for it. And get myself ready, too. My no-air-conditioning days were long behind me. At seventy-two years old, I had no business letting my body get overheated. If service went too long, I would have to tip out.

"I don't know, Mama B." Rev. Martin had sighed, wiping sweat from his forehead already. He led us from the fellowship hall back to the main foyer. "You think we ought to cancel service? It'll start getting real hot around noon."

Mother Pugh shook her head so hard her pillbox hat like ta fell off. "We will do no such thing. This church been open every Sunday for thirty-nine years. We don't cancel service for nothin'. If the flood of '87 didn't stop us, neither will a little sunshine."

"Who's preachin' today?" I had asked him.

His eyes shifted off to the right a little, then he replied. "I believe Rev. Omar, from St. Luke."

Rev. Martin's face winced a bit. I knew he was suffering, trying to run things in his uncle's absence and his aunt's illness.

Our Pastor, Ed Phillips, was hit-and-miss on Sundays since they took first lady Geneva Phillips to get special treatment at that cancer center in Oklahoma.

"How's Geneva?"

His eyebrows raised, he shook his head. "Mama B, I really don't know. Uncle Ed says she's entering stage four."

In all my years, I done heard so many doctors be wrong, terms like "stage four" don't phase me none. "Rev. Martin, don't you be moved by what they say, you keep your aunt lifted in prayer."

"Yes, ma'am."

I looked up at Rev. Martin. Spittin' image of his mother – I used to work with her in the salon. Rev. Martin was still young. In his early fifties. Needed to prove himself a faithful Indian before he took on the title of Chief one of these days—if the Lord ever called him to preach.

Ophelia, Rev. Martin and I entered the sanctuary again through the swinging wooden doors. I took a deep breath. Lord knows I love the smell of His house. The carpet, the pews, the old wooden pulpit Pastor Phillips and my Albert built with their own hands. They set every stained glass window in place, nailed down every pew, laid all the baseboards on top of the carpet. Pastor Phillips wasn't married back then, so I had to look out for both of them. Brought them iced tea and lemonade, fed them after the end of a hard day's work—mostly on Saturdays and Sundays because we all had full-time jobs. Took us a while, but Mt. Zion had been built with a lot of faith, patience, love, and sweat.

Back in '73, when Albert and I donated the other half of our property to build the church on, we knew this space would be something special. A place where folks could come and get help and experience the love of Jesus through His people.

Pastor Phillips really wasn't that good a preacher back then. He used to read from his yellow legal pad like my kids used to read from their little note cards when they gave a speech at school. Nervous! But God anointed Pastor Phillips and used him anyway because he had a willing heart and he loved people. He was a real good pastor before he was a real good preacher. Sometimes, it's like that. God give you grace as you go in faith.

Anyhow, we sure did miss Pastor Phillips' pastorin' and his preachin' while he was out caring for his wife. Rev. Martin was doing a good enough job of holding down the fort, but all those different ministers coming on all those different Sundays was startin' to wear me out. Some of 'em so wired up, felt like we was at a rock and roll show. And some of 'em be 'bout to put me to sleep right there on the front row. I know, I know the Lord just trainin' 'em up like he did Pastor Phillips. I got to be more patient.

But wasn't going to be much patience that day with no air in the building. Already, I could feel my pores opening up, and it wasn't even nine o'clock yet.

I looked at Rev. Martin over the rim of my glasses. "Listen here, I'll pray and ask the Lord to hold off the heat. You tell Rev. Omar to preach real fast today, okay?"

Mama B: A Time to Speak is Available Now!

About the Author

Michelle Stimpson's works include the highly acclaimed *Boaz Brown*, *Divas of Damascus Road* (National Bestseller), and *Falling Into Grace,* which has been optioned for a movie of the week. She has written over twenty books and published more than fifty short stories for high school students through her educational publishing company at WeGottaRead.com.

Michelle serves in women's ministry at her home church, Oak Cliff Bible Fellowship. She also ministers to women and writers through her blog. She regularly speaks at special events and writing workshops sponsored churches, schools, book clubs, and educational organizations.

The Stimpsons are proud parents of two young adults and one crazy dog.

Other Books by Michelle Stimpson

Fiction

Boaz Brown

Divas of Damascus Road

Falling into Grace

I Met Him in the Ladies' Room (Novella)

I Met Him in the Ladies' Room Again (Novella)

Last Temptation (Starring "Peaches" from *Boaz Brown*)

Mama B: A Time to Speak (Book 1)

Mama B: A Time to Dance (Book 2)

Mama B: A Time to Love (Book 3)

Someone to Watch Over Me

Stepping Down

The Good Stuff

Trouble In My Way (Young Adult)

What About Momma's House (Novella)

Non-Fiction

Did I Marry the Wrong Guy? And other silent ponderings of a fairly normal Christian wife

Uncommon Sense: 30 Truths to Radically Renew Your Mind in Christ

Visit Michelle online:

www.MichelleStimpson.com

www.Facebook.com/michelle.stimpson2

15803332R00078

Made in the USA
San Bernardino, CA
06 October 2014